A NEW BEGINNING

THE SPINSTERS GUILD

ROSE PEARSON

D1518969

A NEW BEGINNING: A REGENCY ROMANCE NOVELLA

The Spinsters Guild

(Book 1)

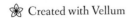 Created with Vellum

A NEW BEGINNING

CHAPTER ONE

"Good evening, Miss Taylor."

Miss Emily Taylor, daughter to the Viscount Chesterton, kept her gaze low to the ground, her stomach knotting. The gentleman who had greeted her was, at this present moment, looking at her with something akin to a leer, his balding head already gleaming in the candlelight.

"Good evening, Lord Smithton," she murmured, hearing the grunt from her father than indicated she should be doing more than simply acknowledging the gentleman's presence. The last thing Emily wished to do, however, was to encourage the man any further. He was, to her eyes, grotesque, and certainly not a suitable match for someone who had only recently made her debut, even *if* he was a Marquess.

"Emily is delighted to see you this evening," her father said, giving Emily a small push forward. "I am certain she will be glad to dance with you whenever you wish!"

Emily closed her eyes, resisting the urge to step back from the fellow, in the knowledge that should she do so, her father would make certain that consequences would follow. She could not bring herself to speak, almost feeling Lord Smithton's eyes roving over her form as she opened her eyes and kept her gaze low.

"You know very well that I would be more than pleased to accompany you to the floor," Lord Smithton said, his voice low and filled with apparent longing. Emily suppressed a shudder, forcing herself to put her hand out and let her dance card drop from her wrist. Lord Smithton, however, did not grasp her dance card but took her hand in his, making a gasp escape from her mouth. The swift intake of breath from behind her informed Emily that she was not alone in her surprise and shock, for her mother also was clearly very upset that Lord Smithton had behaved in such an improper fashion. Her father, however, said nothing and, in the silence that followed, allowed himself a small chuckle.

Emily wanted to weep. It was obvious that her father was not about to say a single word about Lord Smithton's improper behavior. Instead, it seemed he was encouraging it. Her heart ached with the sorrow that came from having a father who cared so little for her that he would allow impropriety in front of so many of the *beau monde*. Her reputation could be stained from such a thing, whispers spread about her, and yet her father would stand by and allow them to go about her without even a twinge of concern.

Most likely, this was because his intention was for Emily to wed Lord Smithton. It had been something

Emily had begun to suspect during these last two weeks, for Lord Smithton had been present at the same social gatherings as she had attended with her parents, and her father had always insisted that she greet him. Nothing had been said as yet, however, which came as something of a relief, but deep down, Emily feared that her father would simply announce one day that she was engaged to the old, leering Lord Smithton.

"Wonderful," Lord Smithton murmured, finally letting go of Emily's hand and grasping her dance card. "I see that you have no others as yet, Miss Taylor."

"We have only just arrived," said Emily's mother, from just behind Emily. "That is why –"

"I am certain that Lord Smithton does not need to know such things," Lord Chesterton interrupted, silencing Emily's mother immediately. "He is clearly grateful that Emily has not yet had her head turned by any other gentleman as yet."

Closing her eyes tightly, Emily forced herself to breathe normally, aware of how Lord Smithton chuckled at this. She did not have any feelings of attraction or even fondness for Lord Smithton but yet her father was stating outright that she was interested in Lord Smithton's attentions!

"I have chosen the quadrille, the waltz and the supper dance, Miss Taylor."

Emily's eyes shot open, and she practically jerked back the dance card from Lord Smithton's hands, preventing him from finishing writing his name in the final space. Her father stiffened beside her, her mother gasping in shock, but Emily did not allow either reaction to prevent her from keeping her dance card away from Lord Smithton.

"I am afraid I cannot permit such a thing, Lord Smithton," she told him plainly, her voice shaking as she struggled to find the confidence to speak with the strength she needed. "Three dances would, as you know, send many a tongue wagging and I cannot allow such a thing to happen. I am quite certain you will understand." She lifted her chin, her stomach twisting this way and that in fright as Lord Smithton narrowed his eyes and glared at her.

"My daughter is quite correct, Lord Smithton," Lady Chesterton added, settling a cold hand on Emily's shoulder. "Three dances are, as you know, something that the *ton* will notice and discuss without dissention."

Emily held her breath, seeing how her father and Lord Smithton exchanged a glance. Her eyes began to burn with unshed tears but she did not allow a single one to fall. She was trying to be strong, was she not? Therefore, she could not allow herself to show Lord Smithton even a single sign of weakness.

"I suppose that is to be understood," Lord Smithton said, eventually, forcing a breath of relief to escape from Emily's chest, weakening her. "Given that I have not made my intentions towards you clear, Miss Taylor."

The weakness within her grew all the more. "Intentions?" she repeated, seeing the slow smile spreading across Lord Smithton's face and feeling almost sick with the horror of what was to come.

Lord Smithton took a step closer to her and reached for her hand, which Emily was powerless to refuse. His eyes were fixed on hers, his tongue running across his lower lip for a moment before he spoke.

"Your father and I have been in discussions as regards your dowry and the like, Miss Taylor," he explained, his hand tightening on hers. "We should come to an agreement very soon, I am certain of it."

Emily closed her eyes tightly, feeling her mother's hand still resting on her shoulder and forcing herself to focus on it, to feel the support that she needed to manage this moment and all the emotions that came with it.

"We shall be wed before Season's end," Lord Smithton finished, grandly, as though Emily would be delighted with such news. "We shall be happy and content, shall we not, Miss Taylor?"

The lump in Emily's throat prevented her from saying anything. She wanted to tell Lord Smithton that he had not even asked her to wed him, had not considered her answer, but the words would not come to her lips. Of course, she would have no choice in the matter. Her father would make certain of that.

"You are speechless, of course," Lord Smithton chuckled, as her father grunted his approval. "I know that this will come as something of a surprise that I have denied myself towards marrying someone such as you, but I have no doubt that we shall get along rather famously." His chuckle became dark, his hand tightening on hers until it became almost painful. "You are an obedient sort, are you not?"

"She is," Emily heard her father say, as she opened her eyes to see Lord Smithton's gaze running over her form. She had little doubt as to what he was referring to, for her mother had already spoken to her about what a husband would require from his wife, and the very thought terrified her.

"Take her, now."

Lord Smithton let go of Emily's hand and gestured towards Lady Chesterton, as though she were his to order about.

"Take her to seek some refreshment. She looks somewhat pale." He laughed and then turned away to speak to Emily's father again, leaving Emily and her mother standing together.

Emily's breathing was becoming ragged, her heart trembling within her as she struggled to fight against the dark clouds that were filling her heart and mind. To be married to such an odious gentleman as Lord Smithton was utterly terrifying. She would have no joy in her life any longer, not even an ounce of happiness in her daily living. Was this her doing? Was it because she had not been strong enough to stand up to her own father and refuse to do as he asked? Her hands clenched hard, her eyes closing tightly as she fought to contain the sheer agony that was deep within her heart.

"My dear girl, I am so dreadfully sorry."

Lady Chesterton touched her arm but Emily jerked away, her eyes opening. "I cannot marry Lord Smithton, Mama."

"You have no choice," Lady Chesterton replied, sadly, her own eyes glistening. "I have tried to speak to your father but you know the sort of gentleman he is."

"Then I shall run away," Emily stated, fighting against the desperation that filled her. "I cannot remain."

Lady Chesterton said nothing for a moment or two, allowing Emily to realize the stupidity of what she had said. There was no-one else to whom she could turn to, no-one else to whom she might escape. The only choices that were open to her were either to do as her father asked or to find another who might marry her instead – and the latter gave her very little hope.

Unless Lord Havisham....

The thought was pushed out of her mind before she could begin to consider it. She had become acquainted with Lord Havisham over the few weeks she had been in London and he had appeared very attentive. He always sought her out to seek a dance or two, found her conversation engaging and had even called upon her on more than one occasion. But to ask him to consider marrying her was something that Emily simply could not contemplate. He would think her rude, foolish and entirely improper, particularly when she could not be certain that he had any true affection for her.

But if you do nothing, then Lord Smithton will have his way.

"Emily."

Her mother's voice pulled her back to where she stood, seeing the pity and the helplessness in her mother's eyes and finding herself filling with despair as she considered her future.

"I do not want to marry Lord Smithton," Emily said again, tremulously. "He is improper, rude and I find myself afraid of him." She saw her mother drop her head, clearly struggling to find any words to encourage Emily. "What am I to do, mama?"

"I – I do not know." Lady Chesterton looked up slowly, a single tear running down her cheek. "I would save you from this if I could, Emily but there is nothing I can do or say that will prevent your father from forcing this upon you."

Emily felt as though a vast, dark chasm had opened up underneath her feet, pulling her down into it until she could barely breathe. The shadows seemed to fill her lungs, reaching in to tug at her heart until it beat so quickly that she felt as though she might faint.

"I must go," Emily whispered, reaching out to grasp her mother's hand for a moment. "I need a few minutes alone." She did not wait for her mother to say anything, to give her consent or refusal, but hurried away without so much as a backward look. She walked blindly through the crowd of guests, not looking to the left or to the right but rather straight ahead, fixing her gaze on her goal. The open doors that led to the dark gardens.

The cool night air brushed at her hot cheeks but Emily barely noticed. Wrapping her arms about her waist, she hurried down the steps and then sped across the grass, not staying on the paths that wound through the gardens themselves. She did not know where she was going, only that she needed to find a small, dark, quiet space where she might allow herself to think and to cry without being seen.

She soon found it. A small arbor kept her enclosed as she sank down onto the small wooden bench. No sound other than that of strains of music and laughter from the ballroom reached her ears. Leaning forward, Emily felt herself begin to crumble from within, her heart aching and her mind filled with despair. There was no way out. There was nothing she could do. She would have to marry Lord Smithton and, in doing so, would bring herself more sadness and pain than she had ever felt before.

There was no-one to rescue her. There was no-one to save her. She was completely and utterly alone.

CHAPTER TWO

Three days later and Emily had stopped her weeping and was now staring at herself in the mirror, taking in the paleness of her cheeks and the dullness of her eyes.

Her father had only just now informed her that she was to be wed by the Season's end and was now to consider herself engaged. There had been no discussion. There had been not even a thought as to what she herself might feel as regarded Lord Smithton. It had simply been a matter of course. She was to do as her father had directed, as she had been taught to do.

Emily swallowed hard, closing her eyes tightly as another wave of tears crashed against her closed lids. Was this to be her end? Married to Lord Smithton, a gentleman whom she despised, and allowing herself to be treated in any way he chose? It would be a continuation of her life as it was now. No consideration, no thought was given to her. Expected to do as she was instructed without question – and no doubt the consequences would be severe for her if she did not do as Lord Smithton expected.

A shudder ran through her and Emily opened her eyes. For the first time, a small flickering flame of anger ignited and began to burn within her. Was she simply going to allow this to be her life? Was she merely going to step aside and allow Lord Smithton and her father to come to this arrangement without her acceptance? Was she truly as weak as all that?

Heat climbed up her spine and into her face. Weak was a word to describe her, yes. She *was* weak. She had tried, upon occasion, to do as she pleased instead of what her father had demanded of her and the punishment each time had broken her spirit all the more until she had not even a single thought about disobeying him. It had been what had led to this circumstance. If she had been stronger, if she had been more willing to accept the consequences of refusing to obey her father without question without allowing such a thing to break her spirit, then would she be as she was now?

"Then mayhap there is a time yet to change my circumstances."

The voice that came from her was weak and tremulous but with a lift of her chin, Emily told herself that she needed to try and find some courage if she was to find any hope of escaping Lord Smithton. And the only thought she had was that of Lord Havisham.

Viscount Havisham was, of course, lower in title and wealth than the Marquess of Smithton, but that did not matter to Emily. They had discovered a growing acquaintance between them, even though it was not often that her father had let her alone to dance and converse with another gentleman. It had been a blessing that the requests to call upon her had come at a time when her father had been resting from the events of the previous evening, for her and her mother had been able to arrange for him to call when Lord Chesterton had been gone from the house. However, nothing of consequence had ever been shared between them and he certainly had not, as yet, made his request to court her but mayhap it had simply been too soon for such a decision. Regardless, Emily could not pretend that they did not enjoy a comfortable acquaintance, with easy conversation and many warm glances shared between them. In truth, her heart fluttered whenever she laid eyes upon him, for his handsome features and his broad smile had a profound effect upon her.

It was her only chance to escape from Lord Smithton. She had to speak to Lord Havisham and lay her heart bare. She had to trust that he too had a fondness for her, in the same way that she had found her affections touched by him. Else what else was she to do?

Lifting her chin, Emily closed her eyes and took in a long breath to steady herself. After a moment of quiet reflection, she rose and made her way to the writing table in the corner of the bedchamber, sitting down carefully and picking up her quill.

"Miss Taylor."

Emily's breath caught as she looked up into Lord

Havisham's face. His dark blue eyes held a hint of concern, his smile somewhat tensed as he bowed in greeting.

"Lord Havisham," she breathed, finding even his very presence to be overwhelming. "You received my note, then."

"I did," he replied, with a quick smile, although a frown began to furrow his brow. "You said that it was of the utmost importance that we spoke this evening."

Emily nodded, looking about her and seeing that her father was making his way up the small staircase towards the card room, walking alongside Lord Smithton. Their engagement was to be announced later this evening and Emily knew she had to speak to Lord Havisham before that occurred.

"I know this is most untoward, but might we speak in private?" she asked, reaching out and surreptitiously putting her hand on his arm, battling against the fear of impropriety. She had done this much, she told herself. Therefore, all she had to do was continue on as she had begun and her courage might be rewarded.

Lord Havisham hesitated. "That may be a little...."

Emily blushed furiously, knowing that to speak alone with a gentleman was not at all correct, for it could bring damaging consequences to them both – but for her, at this moment, she did not find it to be a particularly concerning issue, given that she was to be married to Lord Smithton if he did not do anything.

"It is of the greatest importance, as I have said," she replied, quickly, praying that he would consent. "Please, Lord Havisham, it will not take up more than a few minutes of your time." Seeing him hesitate even more, she bit her lip. "Surely you must know me well enough to know that I would not force you into anything, Lord Havisham," she pleaded, noting how his eyes darted away from hers, a slight flush now in his cheeks. "There is enough of a friendship between us, is there not?"

Lord Havisham nodded and then sighed "I am sorry, Miss Taylor," he replied, quietly, looking at her. "You are quite right. Come. The gardens will be quiet."

Walking away from her mother – who did not do anything to hinder Emily's departure, Emily felt such an overwhelming sense of relief that it was all she could do to keep her composure. Surely Lord Havisham, with his goodness and kind nature, would see the struggle that faced her and seek to do what he could to bring her aid? Surely he had something of an affection in his heart for her? But would it be enough?

"Now," Lord Havisham began, as they stepped outside. "What is it that troubles you so, Miss Taylor?"

Now that it came to it, Emily found her mouth going dry and her heart pounding so furiously that she could barely speak. She looked up at Lord Havisham, seeing his features only slightly in the darkness of the evening and found herself desperately trying to say even a single word.

"It is....." Closing her eyes, she halted and dragged in air, knowing that she was making a complete cake of herself.

"I am to be wed to Lord Smithton," she managed to say, her words tumbling over each other in an attempt to be spoken. "I have no wish to marry him but my father insists upon it." Opening her eyes, she glanced warily up at Lord Havisham and saw his expression freeze.

"I should offer you my congratulations," he stammered, suddenly rubbing his chin with two long fingers. "I am certain that –"

"*Your* attentions, Lord Havisham, have been countlessly more welcomed than those of Lord Smithton." A swell of determination had suddenly ripped through Emily's chest, her hands clenching into fists as she spoke. "I have longed to spend more time with you and would be glad to accept your courtship, should you ever wish to give it."

Lord Havisham said nothing for some moments after this pronouncement, clearly astonished by what she had said. Emily did not look away, her dark future giving her the impetus she needed to speak from the heart. He was, she knew, her only hope.

Clearing his throat, Lord Havisham began to shake his head and instantly, Emily felt all hope begin to flicker and die.

"I will not pretend that I have found your company to be greatly enjoyable, Miss Taylor," he told her, putting his hands behind his back and holding them there tightly. "I had considered that I might seek to court you but now it seems that matters have been taken out of my hands."

Emily swallowed hard, an ache settling in her throat. "There is always Scotland," she whispered, aware that she was sounding desperate but being quite unable to pretend that she was accepting of her situation. "My father might never grant you courtship but we could escape and marry over the anvil." Stepping forward, she put one hand on his arm, grasping it tightly. "Please, Lord Havisham. If you have any fondness for me whatsoever, tell me that you will at least consider my request."

Lord Havisham sighed heavily, let his hands fall to his sides so that he no longer stood tense and taut. Emily let her hand slide down his arm to touch his hand, hearing his swift intake of breath as she did so. Sparks flew from their fingers, their prolonged touch bringing a shower of peace to her soul.

And then, he stepped back.

"I cannot," he stated, pulling his hand away and ending their connection. "As much as I regret that you will be forced to marry a gentleman you care nothing for, I can do nothing to aid you in this, Miss Taylor."

She stared at him, her eyes wide and a faint trembling beginning to wash over her skin.

"Were circumstances different, I would have sought to court you, Miss Taylor," he continued, turning the knife that already pierced her heart. "But I cannot permit myself to do so when I know you are already engaged."

"But it is not of my choosing!" she cried, tears beginning to stream from her eyes unhindered. "You know Lord Smithton, do you not? You know, surely, that he is not a suitable match for me."

Lord Havisham sighed and rubbed at his forehead. "I am aware of Lord Smithton, yes," he replied, heavily. "I am aware that his previous marriage ended with the death of his wife after only a few months, but I am certain that the rumors surrounding her passing are nothing more than idle gossip."

It felt as though someone had kicked her hard in the

ribs. "His first wife?" she whispered, having known nothing of it – but Lord Havisham did not seem to notice her shock.

"I fear that the displeasure and discourtesy that would follow my actions of taking you to Scotland would be too much to bear," he finished, a hint of sadness in his voice. "My family name would hold some disgrace for some time, which might even pass onto further generations. As much as I admit a fondness for you, Miss Taylor, it is not substantial enough to –"

Emily swiped the air with her hand, cutting him off. "You have said more than enough, Lord Havisham," she said, tears still burning down her cheeks as agony tore through her heart. "I can do nothing other than accept my fate. You have made yourself quite clear. I do not need to hear anything more."

"Miss Taylor, please."

She turned away from him blindly, swiping at her tears as she hurried further into the gardens. The darkness welcomed her, pulling her into its embrace as she staggered away from him. He had not done as she had prayed he might. Her belief had, perhaps, been foolish but it had been the only hope she had left to cling to. Now it was dashed to pieces, crushed under the feet of Lord Havisham.

CHAPTER THREE

wo years later

"Well," Emily murmured, walking into her townhouse and feeling a weight roll from her shoulders. "This is certainly more of a delight than I expected."

Over the last two years, Emily had dealt with a great deal of difficulty but had managed to return to society with a sense of strength and determination that she had not had before. Now that she was an independent widow, it meant that she had no need to cower before anyone, whether that be a husband or a father. She had nothing to concern herself with other than her own affairs. It was, she considered, rather freeing.

Having been in London for a little less than a week, Emily had taken to walking in the park for a short stroll every afternoon. Most people glanced at her and then looked away, but for some, their interest had become a trifle more apparent. Some looked once, then looked again, but for longer this time. Emily said nothing to them and they said nothing to her, forcing herself to remain entirely disinterested in anything and everything that was said.

"You have a visitor, my lady."

Emily froze, glove in hand, as she stared up at the butler, who was ready to take said gloves from her.

"A visitor?" she repeated, slowly, her stomach suddenly twisting. "And who might this visitor be, might I ask?" It was most unusual to have someone calling upon her without sending a note around first, particularly since Emily had not been expecting anyone. She had not attended any social gatherings since returning to London and was still trying to find the strength to do so.

"It is Lady Blakely," the butler replied, deftly taking Emily's gloves and then handing her a card in their place. "She did insist on waiting for your return, my lady. I am sorry if I did wrong in allowing her to stay."

Emily shook her head, taking in a long breath and pressing a smile to her lips. "You did nothing incorrect, of course," she told him, seeing him visibly relax. "It is merely that I am little surprised at the visit, that is all."

The butler cleared his throat and inquired, "Would you like a tea tray to be delivered? You must be in need of refreshment after your walk."

"Yes, please, that would be wonderful." Emily moved away, stopping to look at her reflection in the mirror.

Her dark brown tresses were pulled back neatly, although there were a few wisps that needed to be smoothed down. The same green eyes that had stared at her in despair some years ago looked back at her now, except they were filled with a measure of confidence that had Emily lifting her chin just a little. She had managed to live with Lord Smithton for a little over nine months before he had passed away and, in that time, had discovered a way to live that ensured she protected herself from his advances. It had taken a great deal of courage to refuse to do as he had insisted, having been trained to obey without question, but having done so once, she had learned she had the strength to do so again and again. Thus had begun her new life. A life where she had been able to live with some dignity, whilst refusing to give her husband what it was he wanted. Lord Smithton's age had prevented him from slapping any of the consequences he threatened down upon her and so she had found herself quite safe from him. Her confidence had only grown as the days and months had passed, to the point that she now knew that she had nothing to fear from anyone, be it gentleman or lady.

A small smile lifted the corner of her lips, her eyes flashing as she wondered why Lady Blakely had come to call upon her. Most likely it would be to discover why Emily had returned to London. This news would then be spread about to all Lady Blakely's friends and acquaintances, who would chew over this gossip for some time. It did not help that the suggestion had been made that Lord Smithton had sought death due to her stubbornness and insubordination – a claim that had been made all the more painful when Emily had discovered that it had come from her own father.

Setting her shoulders, Emily made her way towards

the parlor, walking as gracefully and as calmly as she could. Opening the door, she stepped inside and immediately saw Lady Blakely rise to her feet, a warm smile on her face that did not quite reach her eyes.

Emily was on her guard at once.

"Good afternoon, Lady Blakely," Emily said, curtsying. She recalled Lady Blakely from when she had been in London as a debutante, although the lady had been acquainted more with Emily's mother than with her herself. "I confess I am a little surprised that you have called upon me this afternoon." Her smile remained, her tone warm, but still, the lady flinched visibly. "You will have to accept my apologies for your wait. I was taking a walk this afternoon."

"As I well know," Lady Blakely replied, with a tight smile. "I have seen you there almost every day this week." She curtsied quickly, before sitting down without Emily's request that she do so. The lady's hair was in tight curls, pulled back from her face, although it was more liberally streaked with white than Emily remembered. A pair of dark grey eyes looked back at her as Emily finally took her seat, narrowing slightly at Emily's cool tone.

"So," Lady Blakely began, as the maid came in with the tea tray. "You have returned to London."

"I have," Emily replied, giving a quick smile towards the maid. "It has been two years since I was last in London but I doubt very much has changed."

Lady Blakely sniffed but Emily busied herself with pouring the tea, her instant dislike of the lady burning within her heart.

"You have lost your husband, I hear."

"I have."

Silence filled the room for some moments. Evidently, Lady Blakely had been expecting Emily to say something profound about the loss of Lord Smithton, or to express regret or sorrow. Emily felt no such emotion and therefore did not feel the need to say even a single word. Lady Blakely coughed quietly as Emily set her tea on the table just in front of her, clearly a little displeased with how Emily had conducted herself.

"You have completed your mourning period then, I presume," Lady Blakely asked, making Emily hold back a sigh. "And now have returned to London to seek another."

Emily laughed before she could stop herself. It was not a light, delicate sound but rather one that was filled with harshness. It grated on even Emily's ears but she did not hold herself back from it.

"I hardly think that my return to society should indicate that I seek out another husband," she told Lady Blakely, plainly. "I have only just found my freedom, Lady Blakely, and do not intend to give it up so easily."

Lady Blakely's eyes narrowed all the more, although Emily caught a flicker of interest in those dark slits. "Your freedom, Lady Smithton? I thought you cared for your husband."

"Then you are mistaken," Emily replied, with a small smile. "I tolerated my husband." She knew full well that this statement would be all around London within a few hours but Emily did not care. She had found a new strength within her and she was not about to start shrinking back from the truth. "I am sorry that he met such an untimely end, of course, but I will not mourn a day longer for him than I am required to, Lady Blakely. Now," She tipped her head and smiled at the older lady. "Do you think that will satisfy you?"

Lady Blakely blinked rapidly, clearly unsure as to what Emily meant. "I came to offer my condolences, Lady Smithton, if that is what you mean."

Emily, who did not believe this at all, managed to suppress a snort of disbelief. "I see," she said, coolly. "Then I thank you for your condolences, Lady Blakely." So saying, she lifted her teacup to her lips and took a sip.

Again, a silence settled across the room that Emily had no consideration to break. Lady Blakely was clearly a little perturbed over how Emily was conducting herself but had no words with which to explain such concern. It was quite clear to Emily that Lady Blakely had come simply to seek out some gossip that she might pass on to her friends, or to discover the truth about Lord Smithton's death, although she had not yet asked about the latter.

"Your husband died from a fall from his horse, I believe."

Taking another sip of her tea, Emily cleared her throat and then held Lady Blakely's gaze. "Indeed," she replied, calmly.

"I did hear," Lady Blakely continued, leaning forward in a conspiratorial fashion, "that your marriage was not a happy one."

There was no answer that Emily was willing to give to such a declaration. Her marriage to Lord Smithton had been greatly unhappy, but there was no need for anyone to be aware of such a thing, and certainly not someone like Lady Blakely. She did not reply, therefore, allowing Lady Blakely's statement to hang in the air and fall to the ground thereafter.

"I can see that I am not going to be successful in any attempt at conversation from you," Lady Blakely said suddenly, putting her teacup down and hurriedly rising to her feet, her skirts billowing out around her. "Goodness, Lady Smithton, you have changed vastly since I last was introduced to you."

Emily could not help but smile. "I am glad to hear it," she told Lady Blakely, seeing the lady start in surprise. "I was a mouse when I first came to London, Lady Blakely. A mouse who was told what to do, how to act, what to say and who to marry." Her confidence filled her chest as she rose to her feet, one eyebrow arching gently. "I am no longer that mouse, Lady Blakely, and therefore even less inclined to allow anyone to try and persuade me to speak about what I do not wish to. Particularly when I am certain that they seek to discover such things from me so that they might then pass it on to others." She saw Lady Blakely's color heighten but did not hold herself back from continuing to speak honestly. "I am aware that there will be some question over my return to London and believe me, I know full well the extent of my father's whispers, but I will not permit such things to pull me down into a pit of despair. A pit from which I have only just escaped, Lady Blakely."

Lady Blakely sniffed and hoisted her chin in the air. "I do not think that you will do particularly well in London, Lady Smithton," she told her, judgmentally. "You have become abrasive in your manner and are now suggesting such things about my own character – that I am here only to seek gossip and such like – when the truth is that I came merely to offer my sympathies to a young lady who now finds herself without her husband."

Emily did not move, nor did she let Lady Blakely's words sting her. She had the measure of Lady Blakely and would not allow her ill manner to affect how she behaved in any way. She was beyond that now.

Seeing that she was to get no reaction from Emily, Lady Blakely huffed loudly, then turned on her heel and walked towards the door. "I bid you good day, Lady Smithton," she said, her voice high pitched and her face turned away from Emily. "I do not think I shall seek out your company again."

And nor shall I, thought Emily, gratefully, as the lady marched from the room. *I shall choose my own acquaintances amongst society, since I am finally permitted to do so, and gossipmongers shall not be amongst them.*

Feeling fairly satisfied with how the visit had gone, Emily rose to her feet and wandered to the window, looking down upon London and thinking back to when she had first arrived as a debutante. Things were vastly different now, particularly as regarded her own character. She had grown in confidence and in strength of mind, able to see that she *could,* in fact, choose her own path in spite of what others might think. That was precisely what she was here to do now. Having no intention of seeking out a new husband, Emily wanted to experience all that London had to offer for what would be the first time in her life. Free from expectations, from demands and from society's urgings, she would go where she pleased and speak to whomever she wished. She would care nothing for what society thought of her, for her reputation meant nothing to them now. She was a widow and had her own means by which to live, which meant that she could do precisely as she pleased.

Emily intended to enjoy every minute of it.

CHAPTER FOUR

*W*alking through St James Park alone was a welcome relief from the crush of last evening. Emily allowed herself to breathe deeply, wanting to spread her arms wide in order to take in the fresh air, the clouds, the sky and the beautiful sunshine. She had attended her first ball of the Season only last night, having been invited by Lord Churston, whom she remembered from her first Season. It had taken Emily some time to consider whether or not she would accept, but in the end, she had done so. The ball had been filled with guests and she had, for the most part, had an enjoyable evening. She had not danced with anyone, however, even though one or two gentlemen had asked. She had seen the look on their faces. They had wanted her to dance simply for the notoriety of dancing with Lady Smithton. It would simply be another way to feed the gossip that was swirling all around London about her.

Emily sighed to herself and tried to push such thoughts from her mind. How different it was now that she was free to behave and to act as she pleased! She was able to speak to those she wished to speak to, to refrain from those she disliked. She could choose whether she wanted to dance or if she should stay away from the dance floor. No-one could tell her what to do.

Of course, there had been a good many questions from those about her as to her current standing in society. It had come as something of a surprise to discover that the new Lord Smithton – a gentle, older man that was a distant relation of her late husband – was willing to not only give her back the sum of her dowry but also to bequeath her a small townhouse in London. She had been permitted to spend her mourning year at the estate and her marital home, before moving to London, and it was this that had surprised many people. Apparently, many had thought that she would now be seeking a new situation with a new husband, so that her current position in life, along with all the good things that came with having substantial wealth, could be continued. Emily had quashed that idea repeatedly, although she had never gone into detail about why she was now able to live with such independence. The *ton* did not need to know such a thing. All that was required for their understanding was to know that she was a lady of independent means who had no intention of giving up her freedom in order to remarry, no matter who it was that proposed.

"My goodness, is that...?"

Tugged from her thoughts by the sound, Emily arched one eyebrow and looked directly at the two young ladies who were whispering much too loudly if they did not want to be overheard. A sigh escaped from her as she did so, finding herself rather wearied by the young ladies' interest and lack of decorum. It was not as though she were not becoming quite used to this sort of thing, given that practically everywhere she went, her presence was noticed. Lady Blakely had done precisely as Emily had expected and had spread the gossip all through London. Emily had overheard some snatches of what had been said, hearing that she had been a hard and cold lady, who had spoken cruelly to Lady Blakely and showed no sadness over the death of her husband. That only gave credence to the other rumor, which still lingered over Emily's head. The rumor that her manner and behavior had been what had driven her husband to take his life.

Not that she was about to allow any such whisperings to go past unnoticed, however! Emily had decided that, instead of simply overhearing gentlemen and ladies commenting about her, she would turn to them and address them directly. It took a good deal of courage and assertiveness, but the first time she had done so, the gentleman who had been speaking had been so ashamed that he had backed away stammering apologies. It gave her the thought that she should continue to do so, in order to prove to the *beau monde* that she was not about to be trifled with.

"I do not think it is," the second young lady said to the first. "Besides which, I –"

"Yes," Emily interrupted, firmly, turning to face the two young ladies. "It is I, Lady Emily Smithton. That is, I am certain, to whom you are referring?" She arched one eyebrow and gave them both a stern glance, which immediately brought about the effect she had hoped.

The first young lady colored at once, her cheeks going a deep scarlet as she turned her head away. It was clear that she was struggling to find something to say, having not expected Emily to turn her head and speak to them about what they had been whispering. The second young lady, however, showed no such strong reaction. Her cheeks colored, yes, but she continued to regard Emily with rather obvious interest. Emily looked back at her directly taking her in. The young lady appeared to be a little older than the first, with a rather dull bonnet and certainly an obvious lack of manners!

"Is there something you wish to say to me?" Emily asked, growing a little irritated with the continued stare of the young lady, who should have been embarrassed enough to have, at the very least, made an apology! "I know that there is a rumor going around London about the passing of my husband but I can assure you that such rumors do not influence me in the slightest. I am also aware that Lady Blakely has decided that I am rude and cold in my manner and so has been speaking of such things to anyone who will listen. Nothing has affected me as yet. Therefore, you are welcome to tell whomever you wish that you have seen me and even spoken to me, if you wish it but pray, desist your gawping!" She arched a brow. "Not only it is unspeakably rude, it is entirely unladylike for two young ladies such as yourselves."

This speech seemed to have affected the second young lady, for she did drop her gaze but, much to Emily's surprise, stepped forward, bobbing into an awkward curtsy right in the middle of St. James' Park. The first young lady did no such thing, hissing urgently at the second who took no notice of her. Emily, surprised, remained where she was, wondering what this young lady thought she was doing.

"I must apologize profusely for my rudeness, Lady Smithton," said the creature before her, now stammering awkwardly. "I- I should not have been staring, nor whispering in such an improper manner, but it is only that I find myself rather in awe of you."

Blinking in surprise, Emily regarded the young lady carefully, taking in her rather sharp features and realizing that she was, in fact, quite tall. The other girl had taken her leave of the first and was now sitting on a bench some yards away from Emily, her face turned away from them both. Emily shrugged inwardly, turning her attention back to the lady in front of her.

"Might I enquire as to your name?" she asked, seeing the color begin to fade from the young lady's cheeks. "We have not exactly been introduced, although you appear to be well acquainted with me."

"Forgive me," the young lady said, quickly, lifting a hand and running it over her eyes. "You are correct to state that I have not been introduced to you." A sharp laugh escaped her. "I am again proving my impropriety and my failings, am I not?" A quick glance was shot towards Emily, who merely stood waiting patiently for her to continue.

The lady cleared her throat. "You attended Lord Churston's ball last evening and I was told then who you were. I will admit that I have heard the gossip and the whispers about you, Lady Smithton, but I have given them no consideration, I assure you." Her eyes darted to

Emily's and, even though she was a little frustrated with the persistence of the young lady, Emily found herself a little concerned at the worry that was etched in the light blue eyes that looked back at her. She was also somewhat intrigued by what this lady meant by speaking to her in such a manner. Was she merely trying to begin an acquaintance? If so, she was going about in the most improper fashion.

"Your name, if you please," she said again, although not unkindly.

"Oh, of course." The young lady scraped into a curtsy again, clearly trying to make up for her previous exhibition of poor manners. "Do excuse me, Lady Smithton. I am Miss Emma Bavidge, daughter to Viscount Hawkridge."

"I see," Emily replied, looking at the young lady but finding no particular nudge in her mind as to who she might be. "I confess that I do not know your name nor that of your father's, Miss Bavidge. Ought I to do so? I was only in London some two years ago but still that name does not come to me."

Miss Bavidge dropped her head, a slow flush creeping up her cheeks. "You have not heard, I suppose," she stated, her fingers twisting together in front of her. "I am a little surprised, for it has been on the lips of almost everyone I know."

Emily frowned, her surprise and her interest growing. "I have only been in London for a fortnight or so, Miss Bavidge. I have not heard a good deal other than my own name being mentioned!" She gave Miss Bavidge a wry smile, feeling as though this young lady was, in fact, speaking the truth about how she had paid little regard to the gossip about Emily. "Pray, do tell me."

Miss Bavidge looked about her helplessly. "Might we walk for a few minutes, Lady Smithton?" she asked, sounding a trifle uneasy. "It can be a heavy burden and walking does aid me somewhat."

A little taken aback by the young woman's quick and apparent distress, Emily nodded and turned to walk along the path again. "You need not fear that I will turn from you, Miss Bavidge," she said, kindly. "Whatever it is that concerns you, it will not bring about my immediate judgement."

The young lady flushed crimson, dropping her golden head. "You are very kind, my lady," she murmured, falling into step beside Emily. "Not everyone is as kind as you, I fear. My father's disgrace has become my own."

Frowning at this, Emily shook her head with a quick understanding and sympathy for what Miss Bavidge spoke of. "If this is what has been troubling you, Miss Bavidge, then be assured that you may speak openly in the knowledge that I will not berate you nor think you shameful in any way. If your father's disgrace is entirely his own doing, then I shall give you none of the blame nor consider your reputation stained beyond hope. Please." She smiled at Miss Bavidge, who had lifted her head a little, seemingly encouraged. "Tell me all that has occurred."

Miss Bavidge let out a long breath, set her shoulders and began to explain and Emily found herself listening intently, feeling as though she had come across someone who might one day, become a friend.

"My father, Viscount Hawkridge, has a penchant for gambling and the like," Miss Bavidge began, regret in her voice. "I will not go into details but he was worried for his fortune due to his great many debts and came across something that he thought he might use to aid him with this trouble." A dark expression flickered across her face. "In short, Lady Smithton, my father attempted to black-mail someone who held a greater position in society than he. This was discovered and revealed, and my father's disgrace was made known."

"And you, also, have been torn down with him," Emily finished, seeing the wretched look on Miss Bavidge's face. "Even though you had nothing whatso-ever to do with the matter. Is that not correct?"

Miss Bavidge nodded, swallowing hard before she replied. "It is exactly as you say, Lady Smithton."

Emily shook her head, her shoulders settling. "That is, I'm afraid, the woman's lot. We are often thrown together with our husbands, brothers or fathers, to the point that their behavior and their rather foolish choices smear us with their own disgrace. It seems quite unfair; do you not think?"

The young lady looked up sharply. "Yes," she said at once, nodding fervently. "Yes, indeed I do. I have a few very dear friends and they treat me very well, I am glad to say."

"Good," Emily said, firmly, wondering to herself if the only reason this young lady had come to speak to her was simply so that she might find herself another ally of sorts. After all, she herself had been tainted by rumors of her late husband's affairs and then subsequent death and it had taken a good deal of inner strength for her to even consider returning to society.

Miss Bavidge cleared her throat, glancing up somewhat awkwardly at Emily, making her aware that the girl had something more to say.

"Yes, Miss Bavidge?"

"Might I....." The young lady trailed off, her face an expression of frustration. "Forgive me. What I ought to say is, if you are so willing, Lady Smithton, might I be permitted to call upon you one day soon? There is something more that I would like to discuss with you, if you would grant me a few minutes of your time."

To Emily's surprise, instead of immediately rejecting the idea, she found herself rather willing to see the young lady again. Whether it was because of the concern in the Miss Bavidge's eyes or because she found their conversation thus far to be rather intriguing, she could not say but, despite all of this, she nodded. "You will tell me then why you think me so admirable, I hope?" she asked, a little teasingly. "After all, you are the first lady I have heard whispering about me, who then promises that they are somehow 'in awe' of me, although I cannot possibly imagine why!"

Miss Bavidge laughed, her face lighting up. "I shall, of course," she replied, eagerly. "I do speak the truth, Lady Smithton, I promise you."

"Then I think I would be very glad if you would call upon me, so that I might understand fully," Emily replied, grinning. "Shall we say early next week?"

Miss Bavidge nodded enthusiastically. "That would be wonderful, Lady Smithton. I cannot thank you enough."

Emily gave her a small, wry smile. "I just hope that I am able to assist you with whatever it is you wish to discuss, Miss Bavidge."

"Oh, I am quite certain that you will be able to, Lady Smithton," Miss Bavidge said with confidence. "I must go, I can see that my friend is waiting for me." Again, she dropped into a curtsy, although Emily was glad to see that she was now smiling instead of appearing nervous and concerned. "Here is my card, Lady Smithton. And thank you."

Emily accepted it with a word of thanks, letting her gaze follow the young lady as she left to return to her friend, who had risen from her seat on the bench. This had certainly been a rather curious encounter, although Emily had to admit to herself that she was certainly intrigued by whatever it was Miss Bavidge wished to discuss with her. She could not help but feel sorry for the lady also, aware that her father, Viscount Hawkridge, must be in a good deal of disgrace at this present moment. Whether or not he had been able to pay what he owed thus far despite his poor attempts at blackmail, she did not know and nor could she guess, but her heart did feel sympathy for his daughter. To be here for the Season, only to discover these horrendous truths about one's father must be incredibly difficult for her. Of course, the *beau monde* might easily turn their back on her even though it was not anything she had done herself – for such was the way of the *ton*. Emily was glad that, at least, this young girl had some friends to speak of and had not been thrown from society entirely although she could imagine that her invitations had dwindled these last few weeks. That made her all the more determined to see the young lady again and do what she could for her.

Feeling a slight chill in the air, Emily sighed to herself as she began to walk back towards the entrance of the park. The *ton* certainly could be cruel, as she herself had discovered. Her husband had died from nothing more than a fall from a horse but within a few hours, it seemed, there had been rumors that he had deliberately thrown himself from it in order to bring his life to an end. It had, as far as she believed, came from her father, whom she had written to almost at once to inform him and her mother of her changed situation. The gossip had sickened her entirely. The *ton* had known, of course, that Emily's marriage to the Marquess of Smithton had been an arrangement made between him and her father, and they also knew just how much Emily's mother had opposed the marriage, albeit in a silent plea instead of any practical measures. After all, the Marquess had been almost twenty-five years Emily's senior.

Why does wealth have such a great impact on the gentlemen of the ton? she wondered to herself, walking slowly back to the entrance to the park. Her father and Lord Smithton had exchanged a good deal of money for her marriage, which she had only discovered once she had been wed for a month or so. The dowry had been given, yes, but Lord Smithton himself had then responded by giving Emily's father a substantial sum in return. Lord Smithton himself had told her this, mocking her one evening when he had been in his cups. She had been bought and sold like she was nothing more than a donkey traded for work.

Lord Smithton had paid for her simply because he wanted a young wife to give him the heir he needed. Given that his previous wife had died early into their marriage, having become a shadow of her former self, the gentility of London were rather wary of him. Nothing more than rumors had been said, of course, but it had been more than enough for the mothers of the *ton* to keep their eligible daughters away from him. Emily's father had done no such thing, however, and had made it clear that he would be willing to marry Emily to Lord Smithton for a price. Emily could still recall how Lord Smithton had laughed in her face, telling her that she meant nothing to her father and was merely a broodmare for him.

That had been the day she had decided to stop allowing herself to be treated in such a degrading fashion. She had withheld everything from the marquess. Since that night, she had refused to leave her quarters and go to his bed, as she was expected to do whenever he called her. His age and his lack of strength had prevented him from chasing her and forcing her to do as he wished, and life had gone on in such a way for a little less than a year. And then, he had died and the rumors had sprung up that he had done so deliberately to escape from his selfish and unwilling wife. They had also whispered that she had found out of his many evenings spent at houses of ill repute and had made his life difficult ever since then when the truth had been quite the opposite. She had never cared what he did, choosing only how to live her own life in as manageable a way as possible, having no respect and certainly no affection for the man she had been forced to marry.

Shrugging to herself, Emily re-tied her bonnet strings and made her way towards the road, hailing a hackney to return her to her townhouse. It was not something she was about to allow herself to linger on, for it had been two years since the event of her marriage and much too long a time to continue dwelling on it. She had to refocus her mind on her present circumstances and find the strength needed to daily rise above the whispers that dogged her heels whenever she stepped out. For the first time in her life, she would seek a life of happiness and contentment, refusing to allow the dull spirit and the weights of the past to continue to bear down on her.

It was time for things to change.

CHAPTER FIVE

"My dear Lady Smithton!"

Emily smiled as graciously as she greeted Lady Clarke, who had once been something of an acquaintance to Emily's mother. However, her own personal consideration of the lady was now markedly different from when they had first met, for Emily was all too aware that Lady Clarke was glad to see Emily present, simply because of the gossip that surrounded her. Lady Clarke would be soon surrounded by those who wanted to know how she was acquainted with Emily and what Lady Clarke thought about the death of Emily's husband – and no doubt, Lady Clarke would be more than delighted to oblige them with her opinions. Yes, indeed, the lady would have a good deal to talk about, and it would all be at Emily's expense.

"How good it is to see you again," the lady continued, looking at Emily with bright, shining eyes and a warm smile. "I have always hoped that you might return to society once you had undertaken your mourning period. How glad I am to see you again!"

"And now, your hopes have been fulfilled," Emily replied, tartly, finding the false tone of Lady Clarke's voice grating on her. "But I should not take up any more of your time."

"Oh, no, do wait a moment!" Lady Clarke exclaimed, putting a hand onto Emily's arm. "I know that you must be finding some aspects of London society to be most troubling." She gave Emily what she presumed to be a sympathetic smile, but Emily remained tight-lipped. "I want you to be aware, my dear, that you can always seek me out and take me into your confidence."

A laugh escaped from Emily's lips before she could prevent it. As much as Lady Clarke appeared to be genuine in her desire to aid Emily, she clearly thought that Emily was something of a simpleton. Did she think that Emily could not see the ladies who were slowly advancing towards Lady Clarke, their eyes fixed upon them both? Did she truly expect Emily to believe that she would keep anything Emily spoke of to herself? Lady Clarke flinched at the laugh that came from Emily's lips, forcing a tight smile to Emily's lips. She wanted to tell Lady Clarke that she would not even consider her offer to be Emily's confidante, but to do so would be more than a little rude and Emily did not want to add to the whispers that were already circulating about her. Instead, she simply chose to ignore Lady Clarke's suggestion entirely, giving it no credence whatsoever. "Thank you for your invitation to your ball, it was very kind of you." She took her arm away from where Lady Clarke held it, her smile never flickering. "Do excuse me. I can see that you have more guests to greet."

She stepped away, leaving Lady Clarke entirely flustered, clearly taken aback by Emily's determined spirit and unwillingness to accept her offer. Emily did not care a jot for what Lady Clarke thought, seeing right through the lady just as she could do with most of the *ton*. That was, of course, the problem with returning to London. One also returned to the lies, the selfishness, the greed, the opulence and, of course, the determination to be more beautiful, more delicate, more refined and elegant than any other – even one's closest acquaintances. Lady Clarke did not care for Emily's state of being, having never once deigned herself to so much as pen a note to her during the two years since Emily had last been in London, so she was not about to accept Lady Clarke's platitudes now.

Letting her eyes rove around the ballroom, she saw many ladies glancing in her direction but chose to ignore them all entirely. She was well aware that she looked more than presentable, in the finest gown of the highest fashion and with seed pearls and delicate flowers being threaded through the dark brown curls of her hair that were piled up high on her head. Yes, she had made sure to look her best this evening, mostly to show the *ton* that she was not affected by their whispers and their gossip, as well as to prove that she was not about to hide in a shadowy corner during such events as this. That was who she had been when her father had first brought her to town, but she would not be so now. She could choose what she wore, where she went and whom she spoke to, instead of being the quiet, fearful young woman that she had been at the first. No, she was a strong and mostly independent young lady, albeit a widow, and that meant more freedom than she had ever had in her life before.

"Lady Smithton! It cannot be!"

Emily turned her head to see a gentleman approach her. He was overly tall, in her opinion, and rather thin, to the point of looking gaunt. His cheekbones were prominent although his small, grey eyes were almost hidden in the depths of his face. Dark brown hair was pulled back from his face, adding to his angular appearance.

"Lord Ralstock, my lady," he murmured, bowing over her hand. "Do you recall? I married – "

"Of course!" Emily exclaimed at once, a flare of heat touching her cheeks as she realized she had quite forgotten him and had only recalled him once he had given her his name. "You married my dear friend Miss Catherine Boyd only a few months after my own marriage." He nodded, a broad smile settling over his features. "I do apologize, Lord Ralstock. It has been some years since I have seen you both although I have always been truly grateful for her letters."

"I know that she has been concerned for you," Lord Ralstock replied, somewhat gravely, his smile fading. "The relief on her face each time she received a response to her letter was evident to everyone who saw her."

Emily smiled gently, her heart filling with contentment over the concern and compassion that the now Lady Ralstock had shown her. Catherine had been one of her only close acquaintances during her first year in town. Whenever she had been able to, Emily had sought her out, although it had not been very often that her father had allowed her to go about societal events alone. Nevertheless, Catherine had written to Emily whenever she could and had informed her about her own marriage. The letters had become less frequent once Emily's mourning period had come to an end, although Emily had informed Lady Ralstock that she would be in London for the Season this year. It would be good to see her again. "Might I ask where Lady Ralstock is this evening?"

Lord Ralstock grinned at her. "She is in confinement, Lady Smithton. That is why her letters have been a little less frequent of late." A slight cloud passed over his face. "She has been very tired indeed."

Emily's eyes widened and, for a moment, she stood there, stunned. "Oh, my!" She shook her head, feeling a lump in her throat that she could not quite explain. "I am truly glad for you both, Lord Ralstock. That is a wonderful event indeed."

The smile returned to Lord Ralstock's face. "I thank you, Lady Smithton. It will be very joyful indeed, I hope." He tipped his head. "She will certainly wish to see you, however." Reaching into his pocket, he pulled out his card and handed it to her. "Might you call upon us soon?"

Emily accepted it at once, nodding fervently and feeling a smile spread across her face. "Oh, yes, of course. Please do give her my regards and tell her I am already looking forward to being reacquainted with her."

Lord Ralstock inclined his head. "But of course. Now, might I present you to some of my acquaintances?

You shall have your dance card filled within minutes, I am quite sure."

Emily let out a small chuckle, thinking he was very kind. "You have not heard of the rumors that follow me about, I presume, Lord Ralstock, else you would not be so eager to be in my company for an overly long length of time."

Lord Ralstock snorted and shook his head, rolling his eyes at her. "I hardly give such things credence, Lady Smithton and nor do I care about what the gossip mongers choose to chew upon. I do not believe for a moment that your character nor your behavior had any influence whatsoever on the death of your husband." He inclined his head for a moment. "Although I was sorry to hear that you had lost him."

A little surprised, Emily felt her lips pull into a smile. "He fell from his horse, having imbibed too much," she said, with a small shrug. "I will not pretend that I had a great affection for him, however, for that cannot be the truth and I will not speak untruths."

Lord Ralstock did not so much as flinch. "I quite understand," he replied, with a sad smile. "It is the way of the *ton*, is it not? Gentlemen do as they please whilst their wives must simply forebear."

"It is," Emily admitted, all the more astonished to hear the understanding in Lord Ralstock's voice. "Lord Smithton was not inclined towards the consideration of others, I confess."

"That is a grave fault indeed," Lord Ralstock replied, his expression sympathetic. "It must have been a trying time for you."

Emily swallowed hard, finding Lord Ralstock's compassion pushing aside the hard outer shell that she had formed about her

"But all the more reason for me to ensure that you have an enjoyable time here in London during *this* Season," he continued, jovially, as though he had seen her struggling to speak openly and did not wish to trouble her further. "Come now, we shall have your dance card filled within the hour, I am certain of it. That is," he finished, with a broad smile, "if that is what you wish."

Emily managed a smile, trying to regain her composure. "That is very kind of you, Lord Ralstock. I confess that I am not certain how many of my acquaintances still remain in London since it has been a few years since I was last present. I did not have a good many acquaintances either, I am afraid since my father was most particular about whom I was introduced to."

"I am certain that a few of your previous acquaintances are present still," Lord Ralstock said, with a chuckle. "Many are now married, of course, but they still come to hear the gossip and the like – which, I'm afraid, you know all too well."

She sighed and nodded. "Indeed I do."

Lord Ralstock shot her a sympathetic smile. "Well then, I shall be careful as to whom I introduce you to, Lady Smithton, keeping you away from those likely to gossip."

Laughing, Emily looked up at him appreciatively. "I thank you, Lord Ralstock. Although I fear it may be an impossible task!"

"Not at all," he said, grandly. "Ah, here we are."

They had come upon a group of gentlemen and ladies, all of whom were talking and laughing together over the noise of the orchestra. Lord Ralstock introduced her to one after the other and she nodded and smiled, ignoring the feelings of anxiety and worry that were growing within her as he did so. Those she was introduced to seemed very proper indeed, for there was no flicker of interest in their eyes as they greeted her, no knowing smiles or anything of the sort to indicate to her that they might be inclined to whisper about her behind her back. Lord Ralstock had done well.

"Ah, and here is Lord Havisham!" Lord Ralstock exclaimed, as a broad-shouldered gentleman stepped forward into the group. "Lord Havisham, this is Lady Smithton."

She could barely lift her eyes to him but forced herself to do so, unwilling to shrink before him as she had done once. Her heart was thundering furiously in her chest as she looked at him, seeing him just she remembered him. The square jaw, the brooding expression, they were all just as she recalled. His fair hair was neatly styled, his blue eyes dark as they regarded her. There was no smile on his face but rather a look of surprise, which was then replaced with something altogether more severe. Emily felt heat climb up her neck but chose to turn away so as not to allow herself to appear embarrassed. Their last meeting had never left her memory, for the shame of it and his harsh words of refusal were burned into her mind. He had not done as she had hoped, had not saved her from the dreadful marriage to Lord

Smithton. Did he regret it now? Or had he turned from his feelings and married another?

"We are already acquainted," she said coolly, lifting her eyes away from Lord Havisham and returning it to Lord Ralstock. "Although thank you for all of your introductions, Lord Ralstock. I am most grateful."

Thankfully, her new acquaintances were eager to further their introductions to her and so a conversation began in earnest. Emily ensured that she did not look back in Lord Havisham's direction as she talked, being quite open and honest whenever there came any questions about her return to London. He would see that she was not the same young lady as he recalled. She was stronger in her spirit now, was determined and certain in her intentions. She had no need to reacquaint herself with him now.

"Yes," she said, in answer to one question. "I was in London some two years ago, when I was first betrothed to the Marquess of Smithton. I am sorry to say that he died only a short time ago. I have just completed my year of mourning."

"But you are still young, Lady Smithton!" one of the younger ladies exclaimed. "I am quite sure that, should you wish it, you will be able to marry again."

Lord Havisham cleared his throat suddenly, making her skin prickle with awareness. Despite her determination, Emily's eyes drifted to Lord Havisham, who was looking back at her with a spark flickering in his eyes.

"No," she said firmly, her gaze now fixed on him. "No, Miss Ruttle. I have very little intention of marrying again, not when I can be a wealthy, independent widow."

She chuckled and looked back at Miss Ruttle. "I may have all the gentlemen in London pursuing me but I shall not be pulled from this life, no matter how much they offer me or how devoted they promise they will be."

There came a shout of laughter at this and Emily found herself smiling with her new acquaintances, although she was well aware that Lord Havisham was not joining in with their mirth. Glancing at him, Emily saw that his gaze was fixed on her, his lips tugging thin and flat with something like regret written in his expression.

"You can still dance, however, can you not?" one gentleman asked, inclining his head. "Might I look at your dance card, Lady Smithton?"

Graciously, she handed it to him and found, to her delight, that the gentlemen now all appeared rather keen to dance with her. She smiled to herself, feeling happiness filling her soul. Perhaps her time in London would be a pleasant experience after all. Perhaps the rumors and whispers would all simply fade away in time – and, most importantly, she would be able to avoid and forget all those who had involved themselves in some way, in her past.

That happiness evaporated in an instant when Lord Havisham, unasked and unwanted, took the dance card from another gentleman and, with a flourish, wrote his name on not one but two of her dances. His eyes lifted to hers, a small smile tugging at the corner of his lips. It seemed she was not going to be able to avoid him after all.

CHAPTER SIX

"*L*ord Havisham."

He bowed and offered her his arm. "Lady Smithton," he murmured, his eyes lingering on hers for a moment.

Memories swamped her as he led her onto the dance floor, his hand settling on her waist as they prepared to waltz. She did not want to feel this. She did not want to recall anything about him or what they had shared together before she had been strong-armed into her marriage to the Marquess of Smithton.

"I did not know you were back in London," he said, softly, as the music began to play.

She stiffened in his arms. "I did not know it was my duty to inform you, Lord Havisham."

His brows furrowed, his eyes darkening. "You are still angry with me."

One of her eyebrows shot up. "Lord Havisham, I did not think you particularly arrogant! I have been away from London for two years and I did not, I'm afraid, spend all that time thinking of you." *Especially not after how you chose to treat me,* she thought to herself, her gaze fixed over his right shoulder. Her heart was hammering furiously despite her outwardly calm and collected appearance and she could only pray that he did not feel it.

"You look somewhat changed since I last saw you," he said in her ear, making her stiffen all the more. She did not want to think about what he meant, all too aware of the heat that was slowly making its way up her spine. When she had first come to London, she had not had any choice in what she wore or how she dressed. Her father had dictated almost everything, much to the chagrin of her mother. She had not been given the best gowns, nor even the highest fashions. Instead, she had been dressed in rather plain, almost dull gowns with only the simplest hairstyles to go with them. That had been because her father had not wished to waste any expenses on a daughter he planned to marry to the Marquess of Smithton, although, at the time, she had not known it. Now that she had wealth of her own, Emily took pride in ensuring she always looked well, choosing to dress in bright colors instead of the dull, washed out tones she had been forced to wear. She said nothing in response to Lord Havisham's remark, tilting her chin a little higher so that she would not even have to look into his eyes.

"Lady Smithton," Lord Havisham murmured, breaking the silence between them. "These last two years have been, for me, filled with nothing but regret. I realize now that I should not have turned away from what was growing between us. I – "

"This is quite unnecessary, Lord Havisham," she interrupted coldly, not wanting to hear another word from his mouth. "You do not need to apologize, nor make any kind of excuse. Believe me when I say that I do not want to hear such things from you."

Lord Havisham did not say another word, much to Emily's relief. Tension flared between them, a cloud settling on Emily's shoulders as she continued to waltz with him. Why had he sought to dance with her when he must surely have known that there could be no delight in renewing their acquaintance?

Closing her eyes for a moment, Emily drew in a deep breath and continued to concentrate on being swept around the floor, making sure not to put a foot wrong. She longed for the music to end, wanting to be free of his grasp so that she could return to her other new acquaintances in the hope that she would be able to regain her sense of calm as well as thrust any thought of Lord Havisham from her mind. She did not want to remember him, did not want to be dragged back into the memories of the past.

"Forgive me, Lady Smithton, but I cannot help but –"

"I believe I have made myself more than clear, Lord Havisham," Emily interrupted, pulling back from him slightly. "Do not press your advantage now, just because we are in close proximity."

Lord Havisham drew in a long breath and shook his head, hearing the music begin to slow in preparation for the last few steps. "I must beg you for the opportunity to speak openly to you, Lady Smithton. My soul has been burning with regret over my behavior towards you the last time we spoke." He looked into her eyes but Emily turned her gaze away, his hand searing through her gown as he continued to hold her tightly. "If only I could be permitted to apologize, then I might find a little relief." His grip tightened around her waist and Emily felt her breath hitch. "Please, Lady Smithton."

The music came to a close and it was with sheer relief that Emily stepped back out of Lord Havisham's arms, curtsying beautifully as she inclined her head. He bowed but let his eyes linger on her as she rose, offering her his arm as they walked from the floor. She did not accept it.

"Must I beg you again, Lady Smithton?" he murmured, as they drew nearer the crowd of guests. "It will only be a few minutes of your time."

She looked up at him as they joined the rest of the guests at the edges of the ballroom. "Your guilt is none of my concern, Lord Havisham. You do not speak of me or the struggles I myself might have gone through and your sorrow over that. Instead, you simply wish to apologize so that *your* guilt might be assuaged." Her eyes narrowed a little, seeing the way he dropped his head, clearly ashamed. "I have nothing to speak to you of, Lord Havisham, nor do I have need to give you any more of my time. Do excuse me."

Not waiting to see if he would reply or had anything else to say to her, Emily moved away from him at once, hating that her pulse was racing as it had done all those years ago. As much as she was hurt by Lord Havisham's request, hurt by his obvious and apparent eagerness to soften his own suffering, she could not help but feel that same strong attraction towards him that had been in her heart some two years ago. He was just as handsome as she recalled, but she could not allow herself to give that any further consideration. It would be best for her to set all that aside and move forward as she had planned. After what she had said to him, Emily had to hope that he would not seek her out again. It was clear she did not wish to continue their acquaintance and Emily prayed that Lord Havisham would respect that. Hopefully, he would not seek her out for their second dance and, if he did, Emily had every thought to refuse him. Picking up a glass of refreshment, she glanced down at her dance card, seeing that she had a few minutes of respite before she had another dance.

"My lady?"

Turning her head, Emily saw yet another young lady to whom she had no knowledge and was certain that they had never been introduced. This particular girl had a long, straight nose with a somewhat square jaw and very little color in her face. Her brown curls hung loosely about her face with very little purpose and her blue eyes lacked any sort of warmth. There was a heaviness about her frame, being broad-shouldered, although she certainly was not in any way rotund. Emily lifted her eyes to the young lady's face, seeing her cheeks now a little pink, clearly aware of Emily's scrutiny.

A nudge of shame bit at her soul. She did not need to look the young lady up and down, and certainly not in such an obvious fashion. "Do excuse me," Emily stammered, feeling a little off-balance. "I was just trying to recall your name."

"Oh," the young lady said, in a quiet voice, her eyes

darting from here to there. "I see. I apologize, of course, but I thought to come and greet you without having made a formal introduction."

"Indeed," Emily murmured, a little surprised that this was now the second time such a thing had occurred, given that the first had been when she had been walking in the park.

The young girl nodded, her hands clasping in front of her. "I have a dear friend, Miss Bavidge, and it was she who encouraged me to become acquainted with you this evening. If it had not been for her reassurance that you would not turn from me then I would not have dared come to speak to you in such a rude manner. I know we have not been introduced and I must apologize for my unexpected interruption."

It took Emily a moment to recall that Miss Bavidge was none other than the first unknown young lady whom she had met only that afternoon. She then allowed a slight smile to cross her face, so as to reassure the girl who was now looking at her with a somewhat strained expression.

"I quite understand," she murmured, tilting her head just a little to regard this new stranger a little more. "Then might I inquire as to who you are?"

The young lady did not smile but rather cleared her throat before inclining her head as though in greeting. "Miss Sarah Crosby," she said, in a bland tone. "My father is Viscount March."

The name did not mean anything to Emily, who simply nodded and accepted this information. "I am glad to make your acquaintance, Miss Crosby," she replied, as the girl lifted her head. "May I now ask why you have sought me out?"

Miss Crosby took in a deep breath. "I know that Miss Bavidge is planning to come and see you very soon," she said, haltingly. "Might I be permitted to join her?"

This perplexed Emily who, looking at the young Miss Crosby, felt all the more confused as to why such a person would seek out her acquaintance. Miss Bavidge, perhaps, sought it so as to know how to deal with the rumors and gossip that were swirling around both her and her father, but why should Miss Crosby seek out a closer acquaintance?

"You are not tainted by gossip also, are you?" she inquired, frowning just a little.

The lady shook her head. "No. I am not."

"Then why – "

Emily found herself cut off by the appearance of one Lord Sutherland, who had come to take her to the dance floor for the quadrille. She had no time with which to speak with Miss Crosby further, quite sure she would lose her in the crowd by the time she returned from the dance.

"Very well," she said quickly, as Miss Crosby's face finally lost some of its dull visage. "You will be welcomed along with Miss Bavidge, of course. I will ask Miss Bavidge to inform you of our arrangement. I will expect you both."

Miss Crosby nodded, although still, she did not smile. "Thank you, Lady Smithton," she said, as Lord Sutherland bore Emily away. "You are very kind."

Still entirely mystified as to why she had not only one

but two young ladies seeking to come and call on her, Emily pushed the matter from her mind and focused entirely on Lord Sutherland and the quadrille, thinking that, aside from Lord Havisham, this had been a truly wonderful evening. She had managed to rise above the gossip and whispers, had been introduced to some members of the *ton* who did not seem to care about her late husband's death and now had something of a mystery with which to occupy her mind.

At least, she thought to herself, wryly, *I will have no reason to think of Lord Havisham again. All I need concentrate on is Miss Bavidge and Miss Crosby. He does not even need to enter my thoughts.*

CHAPTER SEVEN

It was with great curiosity that Emily regarded Miss Bavidge and Miss Crosby as they sat to take tea with her the following Monday afternoon. They were very dissimilar in both stature and features, for Miss Bavidge was slim and tall, with thin features and sharp eyes, whereas Miss Crosby seemed to slump in her chair, with no expression of delight or even interest in her eyes.

"Now," she began, crisply, once they both had their tea with them. "What is it that you are so urgently wishing to speak to me about?"

Miss Bavidge glanced at Miss Crosby, her cheeks paling a little. Miss Crosby gave a slight shrug, as though resigned to whatever it was her friend had planned, before returning her attention to her teacup.

"Do say *something*, Miss Bavidge!" Emily exclaimed, growing a little exasperated with the silence that was stretching across the room. "This has been intriguing me ever since we first met and I confess that I have been vastly interested to know why two young ladies such as yourselves are so eager to make my acquaintance."

Miss Bavidge cleared her throat, set her cup down and folded her hands in her lap.

"And it is very good of you to invite us to your home, when you do not know us in any way and certainly when we were both rather rude in seeking introductions," she said, softly. "The truth is, Lady Smithton, we are both eager for your help."

Emily nodded slowly, a slight frown pinching her brow. Had not Miss Crosby said she was not caught up by rumors and the like? "You wish to know how to deal with the rumors and the gossip mongers, whereas Miss Crosby...." She turned her attention to the other young lady but found herself a little lost. "Why are you here, Miss Crosby?"

Miss Crosby shrugged indelicately. "Because it is as Miss Bavidge has said. We are both eager for your help."

A niggle of annoyance had Emily's frown deepening. She returned her attention back to Miss Bavidge, who was glancing this way and that, looking now a little pale. "My help in what way, Miss Bavidge?"

The girl bit her lip for a moment. "The truth is, Lady Smithton, we are both entirely without hope. Neither of us have any suitors whatsoever and very little chance of securing one either."

Emily hesitated for a moment, before regarding them both again with a great deal more consideration. "Am I to understand that you are seeking my aid to secure a husband?"

Miss Bavidge nodded fervently, whilst Miss Crosby

sat motionless, her tea now entirely forgotten as it sat on the table in front of her.

"You were very successfully wed to a Marquess, and have then returned to society, entirely transformed," Miss Bavidge said, sounding almost filled with awe. "You have, from what I have heard, become a true beauty and now traverse society's waters with ease," Miss Bavidge continued breathlessly. "Might you, in your wisdom, be able to help us?"

Emily sat back in her chair in a less than ladylike fashion, having been completely taken by surprise. This was not what she had thought Miss Bavidge had come to ask her about at all! She was not simply to issue advice on how to ignore gossip and hold one's head up high throughout it all but, if she was correct in her understanding, was to attempt to find these young ladies a husband! The seriousness of the matter began to hit her, hard. These two young ladies would both be spinsters very soon, if she did not aid them, but what did she know of society and how to pull a gentleman's interest towards oneself? She had not been able to do so with Lord Havisham! When she had needed him the most, believing him to feel that same strong affection as she, he had turned away from her. No, she had no great skill in drawing the attentions and affections of a gentleman!

"I think we have made a mistake coming here, Miss Bavidge."

Before Emily could say anything, Miss Crosby, who had been mostly silent until this point, rose to her feet and gave her friend a pointed look. Miss Bavidge blushed furiously and rose also, stammering an apology and, together, they began to make their way towards the door. It seemed Emily' silence had discouraged Miss Crosby to the point that she now wanted to leave in order to drag the remains of her dignity with her.

Recovering herself a little, Emily managed to halt their progress. "I say, Miss Crosby, whatever gave you the impression that I wished you to leave?"

Miss Crosby and Miss Bavidge turned towards her at once, although Miss Bavidge was the only one who began to turn back towards her seat. Miss Crosby, however, did not even look in that direction, turning to face Emily and regarding her with a sharp eye.

"To be frank, Lady Smithton, you appear shocked rather than pleased at Miss Bavidge's request and your lack of an immediate response gives me in mind that you are likely to refuse us. To save us further embarrassment – which we already have a good deal – I think it best to leave your home and bid you farewell."

Emily watched Miss Crosby carefully and saw, for the first time, a flicker of anguish in her otherwise dull expression. The girl had become well used to hiding what she felt from others, it seemed, but Emily could still make it out. Miss Crosby was desperate enough for Emily's help that she had sought her out at Lady Clarke's ball without introduction but now was ready to leave without more than a moment's notice. Was it shame that motivated her? Or was she speaking the truth when she stated that she believed Emily had been about to refuse them? Emily swallowed hard, feeling a swell of sympathy for Miss Crosby. There was more to this lady than was being immediately revealed and Emily found that she did not want to immediately turn Miss Crosby away, tugging hope from her as she did so. No, instead she wanted to find a way to aid them in whatever way they wished.

"Please," she said, rising to her feet and extending a hand towards Miss Crosby. "Please do come and sit down again, Miss Crosby." She smiled at the young lady and watched with relief as she did as Emily asked, albeit with some degree of hesitation. "You have taken me a little by surprise, that is all. From what I understand, you are asking me to help you find husbands when, I confess, I am not exactly a matchmaker!"

Miss Bavidge, who had been lingering somewhere between Miss Crosby and the chair, now hurried back to her seat with an earnest expression on her face. "Oh, but you have so much more experience that we do, even though we are not exactly in our first flush of youth!"

Emily frowned, seating herself again. "You cannot be on the shelf yet."

Miss Crosby cleared her throat as she sat down rather primly. "I believe we are very close to being referred to as 'spinsters', Lady Smithton. You are well aware, I am sure, that society does not take kindly to young ladies who reach twenty years of age without securing a partner for themselves. I'm afraid we shall both be on the shelf very soon."

"And that does not please you?" Emily asked, reaching to pour them all another cup of tea.

Miss Bavidge's lips trembled. "My father is, as you know, quite disgraced and I have no mother to speak of. My elder brother is already married and settled and will, of course, inherit the title but he has very little time for me. If I do not marry, I shall have to become a companion or a governess and with my father's dirt-splattered reputation, I fear that I shall not easily find a position."

"And I have no-one to turn to," Miss Crosby said, speaking quietly yet firmly, as though she wished to get through the facts without feeling one single emotion. "My father, Viscount March, cares very little for me and has threatened to marry me off to some decrepit old gentleman if I should not find myself a suitable match by this time next year." She shook her head, her eyes dimming all the more. "I am well aware I am not the daintiest of creatures, nor even beautiful, but I cannot abide the thought of being joined with a skeleton of a man for the remainder of my days!"

Emily, who knew well what it was like to marry a much older gentleman, suppressed a shudder. "Indeed," she murmured, quietly. "Whilst I do understand your predicaments and do truly wish to help you, I confess that I do not understand what it is you wish me to do. You state that I have a good deal more experience than you both, but that is not the case. My own father behaved in much the way your own father is threatening, Miss Crosby. I was wed to someone whom I did not care for, in the knowledge that I would have no opportunity to make my own decision as regarded my future."

Miss Bavidge's face fell. "We seek any guidance or aid," she said, hopelessly. "We are both failing terribly, Lady Smithton, and have no-one else to turn to."

"You say that you have no great experience, Lady Smithton," Miss Crosby added, drawing Emily's attention. "But that cannot be the case. You may have been married as you stated, but you have returned to London an entirely new person. From what I understand, at least." She shot a glance towards Miss Bavidge, who began to nod enthusiastically. "You have the ability to rise above the whispers and the rumors that circulate about you. You manage to walk through society with an air of grace and determination that both Miss Bavidge and I lack. Gentlemen seek you out because of it and you are able to refuse them, should you so wish it." Pausing for a moment, Miss Crosby took in a long breath and swallowed hard. "I barely have anyone so much as glancing at me, Lady Smithton, and know no other in society who would be willing to spare their time in order to help me further. When Miss Bavidge told me that you were willing to meet with her, despite her rude interruption and lack of formal introduction, I will admit that it gave me a spark of hope that I have not had in some time."

Emily closed her eyes for a moment. She knew what she *could* do, for she could simply meet the ladies regularly and help them both with their appearance, manners and ability to withstand gossip and the like, but other than that, what else could she do? She did not know a good many gentlemen within the *beau monde* and as such, could not direct them towards Miss Bavidge and Miss Crosby. Although, if Emily continued through the Season, then she might be able to further her acquaintance and thereby, be able to suggest suitable gentlemen for these two young ladies. She would have to get to know Miss Crosby and Miss Bavidge a little better also.

"You are the talk of London," Miss Bavidge said, interrupting her thoughts as her words tumbled out of her in an almost frantic manner. "Almost everyone knows who you are and whilst I know it is not for the best of reasons that they are aware of such a thing, it does make the number of your potential acquaintances grow rather large."

"And you think I could discover which gentlemen are suitable and then introduce you to them," Emily said, slowly, thinking that Miss Crosby had spoken the very thoughts that had been chasing each other through her mind only seconds before. "I can see the hope that you have, Miss Bavidge, although I cannot be certain that I am the one who is best able to help you."

"We have no other," Miss Bavidge replied, quietly, her voice filled with emotion. "There is no-one within our own family to aid us and certainly none within the *ton* would be willing to do so. Yet, I will understand completely if you do not wish to pursue matters with us. We do not know you and you do not know us. I would not have any guilt in your heart over our situation, Lady Smithton. Whatever you decide, I am truly grateful that you were willing to listen to us both."

Emily accepted this quietly and looked into the faces of Miss Crosby and Miss Bavidge, feeling her heart fill with sympathy for them. Surely she could do *something* to help them both, even if it was merely providing a friendship that they could depend on?

"Very well," she said, after a moment, only for Miss Bavidge to gasp with delight and Miss Crosby press one hand to her mouth, tears suddenly sparkling in her eyes. "But I must do a little more thinking on the matter before I decide *exactly* what will take place."

Miss Bavidge nodded, her lips curving into a grateful smile as she, along with Miss Crosby, battled tears.

"Thank you, Lady Smithton," she said, hoarsely. "With all of my heart, I thank you. You do not know what you have done for us."

Emily smiled back at her, already feeling a growing kinship with them both. "But of course," she replied, warmly. "I am quite sure that very soon, I will see you both happy and settled. You need not struggle alone any longer."

Miss Crosby stifled a sob, her gratitude evident as Emily got up to ring the bell for more tea. She could not speak but nodded enthusiastically in the direction of Miss Bavidge, clearly wanting Emily to understand that she too was overcome with thanks. Emily, a little surprised by the strength of the girl's emotion and realizing just how much Miss Crosby held below the surface, gave her a warm smile.

"A little more sustenance, I think," she said, as Miss Crosby pulled out a lace handkerchief and dabbed at her eyes. "We shall become firm friends by the end of this afternoon, I am sure of it. Now, Miss Bavidge, why do we not begin with you? Tell me all you can about yourself."

CHAPTER EIGHT

"*L*ady Smithton."

She did not smile. "Lord Havisham."

The afternoon was fine and Emily had, as she usually did, taken a walk in the park. She did not care for a companion for she was more than content to walk alone, but now it seemed, Lord Havisham was determined to be by her side.

"It is a very fine day, is it not?"

Emily wanted to roll her eyes at such blandness of conversation but instead simply pasted a smile on her lips. "Indeed it is, Lord Havisham," she stated, firmly. "A fine day for walking." She allowed one eyebrow to arch gently. "If you will excuse me, Lord Havisham."

He did not move nor make any attempt to remove himself from standing directly in her path. "Might I join you, Lady Smithton?"

Emily did not want to particularly be in such close quarters with the gentleman who had brought such pain to her heart for so long and nor did she want to be forced into his companionship when she had made her mind up not to think on him for any particular length of time. "I think not, Lord Havisham."

"A short stroll only," he said, sounding a little desperate. "I confess, Lady Smithton, I find your lack of response to my desperation to speak openly to you to be burning in my heart. You know that there is a good deal that I wish to say."

The look in his eyes forced a stab of compassion into her heart, even though she did not want to feel such an emotion for him. "We have discussed this matter briefly already, have we not, Lord Havisham?" she said, arching one eyebrow at him. "I believe I made myself quite clear."

Lord Havisham inclined his head, looking more than a little frustrated. "I well understand your frustration with me, Lady Smithton," he admitted, softly. "I understand your reasons for wishing to remain away from my side. I will not pretend that the dart you threw at me the last time we spoke has not pierced my heart."

Emily remained precisely where she was, recalling just how firmly she had spoken to Lord Havisham when he had begged her for a few minutes of her time after their dance at Lady Clarke's ball. No matter his desperation, no matter his urgency, she did not want to give him the opportunity he desired. All that had been between them was gone now. There was no friendship any longer; there was barely even an acquaintance. She needed nothing from him.

"You stated that my desire to speak to you was simply due to my own selfishness," Lord Havisham began, looking at her carefully, his jaw firm. "That I wished only to cure my own heart of its sadness and guilt. Is that not so?"

Emily sighed inwardly and closed her eyes for a moment, hoping that she was communicating her frustration in an easy and apparent manner. "It is," she replied, tightly. "And I will not turn away from that statement, Lord Havisham, no matter how much you might wish me to do so. I still fully believe that your only aim in speaking to me is simply to assuage your own sense of guilt – although why you should feel such a thing is quite beyond me."

Lord Havisham let out a long hiss of breath between his teeth, running one hand over his forehead as though to ease the pain there. "You have become very blunt in your manner of speaking, Lady Smithton."

She did not accept this as either a compliment or a criticism. "I hardly think that my character should be of any concern to you, Lord Havisham," she told him, trying to ensure that no color rose in her cheeks, no outward expression of her inner frustration was shown. "And again I would state that I believe your urge to speak to me so is simply so that your heart might, once again, be free." A shoulder lifted in a gentle shrug. "Whether it is true that your regret what passed between us during our final conversation together, I cannot say and nor do I wish to know. There is no need for me to consider it now, Lord Havisham. That is all in the past and that is precisely where I wish to leave it."

Lord Havisham said nothing for a moment or two. His blue eyes bored into hers, his breath quick as he held her gaze. Then, he turned his head, looking as though he were about to take his leave, only to step forward and grasp her hands in his.

Emily, utterly astonished by his action, could do nothing more than stare up into his face, her hands limp in his. All at once, Lord Havisham's eyes began to blaze with fire, his face coloring slowly as he leaned down over her. She could not move, could not speak. The intensity of his gaze seared her very soul and brought back all of the emotions she had been urgently suppressing. Her feelings for Lord Havisham, long buried, began to grow again but Emily fought them back with an effort.

"There is more to my regret than what I show, Lady Smithton."

Lord Havisham's voice was harsh, his words urgent.

"I have not wanted to share this truth with you for fear that it will haunt me for the rest of my days should I speak it aloud, but I can see that I have no other hope other than to speak honestly." Closing his eyes for a second, Lord Havisham took in a long breath, his fingers tight on hers. "I have never been able to forget you, Lady Smithton."

Emily drew in a ragged breath, trying to find some semblance of composure but struggling to make sense of all that she felt. Lord Havisham's presence was powerful and strong, forcing her to look up at him and accept what he was saying, even though she did not want to listen.

"The regret that I speak of came upon me the day I turned away from you, Lady Smithton. Had I been wiser, had I been willing to admit what I felt and had the courage to do as you had asked, then how different things might be for us both now!"

Emily's eyes lifted to his, despising the sudden twisting in her stomach. Her mind sought out the possibility of what might have been between them, even though she knew she was being foolish even to think of it. Her heart was beating quickly, her hands seeming to settle in his grasp.

Her mind went back to the first time she had seen him. Lord Havisham had always been a remarkably attractive gentleman and, despite being quite unwilling to admit it, she could remember the day she had first laid eyes on him all those years ago. He had been smiling then, however, a smile that was warm and friendly, with an open expression as he had come to greet her. His friend had been acquainted with her father and they had soon found themselves introduced – and how flattered she had been when he had asked her to dance! They had barely been able to take their eyes from one another and so had started a wonderful friendship. A friendship that she had hoped might lead elsewhere, and might save her from her terrible future of a marriage to Lord Smithton.

But no, he had failed her. Once it seemed that he would have to fight for the right to take her as his wife, he had stepped away before the battle had even begun. She had shed a good many tears over him – which her mother had deeply sympathized with, but which her father had warned her to wipe away or else it would be all the worse for her. At the time, she had wept over the realization that, if only Lord Havisham had loved her enough to face up to her father, to demand that he, not a marquess, marry her, then she would not have to marry Lord Smith-ton. The sorrow that Lord Havisham had brought her with his actions was too large to simply ignore now. Shame crashed over her as she recalled how she had begged him to take her to Scotland, to be married over the anvil, but he had only shaken his head, telling her that it was impossible.

That was the last day she had seen him. That very week, the banns for her marriage to Lord Smithton were called and she was resigned to her fate. Could it truly be that he regretted ever stepping away from her? And if that was so, then what did it mean for her now?

"Lady Smithton," Lord Havisham said, sounding somewhat anxious as though he knew this was his one opportunity to speak his truth from the heart. "I confess that I was wrong to step away from you as I did all those years ago. I have never had any peace over my actions for my heart has always been caught up with none but you."

Her gut twisted.

"I do not wish to hear your apologies, Lord Havisham, as I am sure I have made clear to you on more than one occasion," she managed to say, feeling a spark of anger flare in the middle of all her other swirling emotions. She had asked him not to speak, had not permitted him to give her his apologies, and yet he was doing precisely that. He clearly hoped that, once he had begun to speak, she would not be able to turn from him, would not be able to have him silenced. Angry, Emily looked down at their joined hands, wondering why she simply could not pull her hands from his.

He cleared his throat and she glanced up at him, seeing his sorrowful expression.

"And yet, despite this, Lady Smithton, I will finish what I have begun," he told her, his voice soft and broken with emotion. "It is not to bring relief to my soul, as you think, for regret will be my constant friend until the very end of my days." His eyes were fixed to hers again and Emily found her mouth going dry, her mind questioning what Lord Havisham wished to say. Despite her determination to remain strong, to remain turned away from him, she found that she could not do as she wished. The urge to hear what he wanted to say grew in spite of her anger. With Lord Havisham, she was weak.

Lord Havisham took in another long breath and then dropped his head, no longer looking into her face. "I will confess to you my own foolishness, Lady Smithton. On the day you sought me out, I behaved so foolishly that not a moment goes by that I do not wish to go back to that moment in order to change my actions." His voice was low now, quiet and difficult for her to hear. "I was weak. I was a coward. I did not do what I should have done, Lady Smithton."

At least they could agree on *that,* Emily thought to herself, trying not to let her dignity crumble in the face of his honest brokenness. He did not need to know that his words and his presence were having such a profound effect on her. Nor did he need to know that her heart was filled with such tumbling, tumultuous emotions that she could barely keep it from exploding from her chest. "No," she agreed, crisply. "No, you certainly did not, Lord Havisham. I believed you were fond of me. I believed that there might be something so wonderful between us that our happiness could be made complete." A brittle laugh escaped her. "How wrong I was."

There was a moment of silence.

"You cannot know the depths of my torment ever since that day," he said slowly, pain in every word. "I cared for you deeply and believed truly that you cared for me and yet, due to various circumstances, I turned my back on you."

"Varying circumstances?" she queried, sharply, looking up at him with a slightly narrowed gaze. "Is that because the notoriety that would have come with marrying over the anvil would have been too much for you to bear?" She could not help but allow herself to speak with harshness to her tone as the memories of that night began to flood her.

Lord Havisham flushed but nodded. "I am ashamed to admit to you that what you have stated was part of the reason for my refusal, Lady Smithton," he told her, honestly. "You will recall that I had just come into my title and was doing my best with the estate my father had left me. I feared that, in following after you, in taking you to Scotland, that I would bring a shame to my father's title and heritage. It was entirely wrong of me to think only of myself, Lady Havisham, but I made my choice. Would that I could change it now."

Closing her eyes, Emily slowly pulled her fingers away from his, finding that her heart had begun to settle into a slightly calmer rhythm. He had spoken to her of what he wished and now there was no need for her to continue the conversation any longer.

"Regret will continue to torture your soul, Lord Havisham," she replied, not unkindly. "I have set the past aside and shall no longer allow it to penetrate my thoughts nor my mind at this present moment. What has gone before has been both painful and sorrowful but I will not allow it to intrude on my circumstances now." As she threw him a glance, she saw that he had gone a deep shade of red, clearly ashamed of his past behavior or perhaps struggling with the consequences that came with speaking with such honesty. She cleared her throat gently and turned her head away. "I have discovered a life now that can never be taken from me by another," she finished, untying her bonnet strings in order to simply retie them, by way of keeping her hands busy. "And I believe our acquaintance need do nothing more than come to a quiet end."

"You do not wish to continue our acquaintance?" Lord Havisham asked, sounding a little surprised which only succeeded in irritating Emily somewhat. "I am sorry that it has taken me this long to apologize for what I did – and for what I did not do. You cannot know the depths of my regret."

"Your belated apology has nothing to do with my lack of eagerness to continue as we once were, Lord Havisham," she retorted. "Nor do I have any sympathy for you."

"Sympathy?"

A flush crept up into her cheeks as Emily felt her anger beginning to flare again. "Your regret is nothing to what I have endured."

Lord Havisham's eyes flared with understanding and

he turned his head away, nodding quickly. "Of course, it is not," he said, slowly. "I can only apologize again, Lady Smithton, if you believe me to have made light of it."

Emily sighed heavily, far too aware that she felt something more than she ought for this gentleman. Despite the flickering anger, despite the frustration and the sorrow, she still had a heart that longed to pursue him again. It was a ridiculous emotion to have, given that she had no desire to continue her acquaintance with him nor to listen to another word of his apologies and regrets.

"You had to marry the Marquess after all, then," he continued, quietly, his voice without intonation. "Did you not have any happiness in that, Lady Smithton?"

Her eyes flared as she looked up at him, her hands dropping to her sides as she finished tying her bonnet strings.

"No, Lord Havisham, indeed not," she stated, stiffly, seeing the way he closed his eyes tightly, as though evidence that he was overcome with regret. "I did not find any happiness in being married to a gentleman who was ages with my father and who wished to use me for nothing more than his own pleasures. I did not find happiness in attempting to escape him whenever I could, ignoring his increasingly angry demands for him to be allowed to use me in any way he wished. That is where I had to learn to be strong, Lord Havisham. My husband drank too much and cared too little. I did not mourn him when he died and yet, despite that, I then had to contend with the rumors and gossip flying all over England about his death. Even now, after retreating to the country for my mourning period, I return to London to hear more of the same - although at least I am easier able to manage it." Her mind drifted back to Miss Bavidge and Miss Crosby, who had been so grateful for her assistance. The only reason they had come to her to request her help was because of her notoriety, although she would not admit that to Lord Havisham. A quiet swell of gladness settled over her, pushing aside all other emotions. She had purpose here now. She did not need to consider Lord Havisham or any other gentleman for that matter. Miss Bavidge and Miss Crosby needed her aid and that, Emily knew, would keep her more than content.

Lord Havisham dropped his gaze to the ground, his head bowing low. Emily watched him for a long moment, her anger fading away into nothing. Her marriage to the Marquess could not be entirely blamed on Lord Havisham, of course, for it had been her father's doing entirely. Even if Lord Havisham had attempted to stand up to Emily's father and had demanded that she be permitted to wed him instead of Lord Smithton, Emily knew that he would not have succeeded. He had not the funds that the Marquess had, and her father had always been led by his love of money. Their only choice had been to escape to Scotland, but he had chosen not to do so.

"But enough, Lord Havisham," she said softly, her frustration dying away as she saw him look at her. "Enough has been said. Enough has been done. Let us put the past behind us and continue on as we are. We need not remember the past any longer. You need not be a part of my society life and I need not be in yours. Good day to you." And, so saying, she turned on her heel and walked away from him, finding that her mind was so filled with thoughts and her heart so heavy with emotions that it was all she could do to keep her back straight and her head up, her vision blurring with sudden, unexpected tears.

He had quite undone her.

CHAPTER NINE

*E*mily did her very best to forget about every single word Lord Havisham had spoken to her but found that, in the coming days, she had been unable to push him from her mind. Lord Havisham was charming, handsome and kind – which should be every young lady's hopes when it came to securing a husband – and yet, she told herself, she had no desire to marry again and certainly no desire to reacquaint herself with the one gentleman who had turned from her. She had told him outright that they need not continue their acquaintance, that there was no need to seek one another out when in polite society, and yet the more she thought of it, the more she realized that this was precisely what she wanted.

It was a very strange circumstance in which to find oneself. It was as though she had stepped back into the past and returned to that time when she and Lord Havisham had found a deep friendship and a closeness that she had hoped would lead to something more, except that this time, it was she who was stepping away from what they had built together instead of Lord Havisham himself. Her mind was confused, her heart wanting to be free to feel all the emotions and fondness that were rising up within her all over again but still, Emily pushed them back.

"I am being quite ridiculous," she murmured aloud, walking gracefully into Lord Henderson's townhouse and being greeted by the waiting butler and footmen. After a few minutes of preparation, she was directed to the drawing room which, she saw, was a large, grand room with a good deal of beauty about it.

"Lady Smithton!"

Her host came over to greet her at once and Emily could not help but smile. She had been introduced to Lord Henderson by Lord Ralstock and had found Lord Henderson to be charming, polite and not at all inclined towards gossip. That, in her eyes, made him one of the most exceptional gentlemen of her acquaintance.

"Thank you for inviting me this evening, Lord Henderson."

"Not at all, not at all!" Lord Henderson replied enthusiastically, as he smiled broadly at her. "I believe you will have a good many acquaintances here this evening, Lady Smithton. Although some may be more eager to know you than you are to know them, unfortunately." A small, frustrated smile crossed Lord Henderson's face, telling Emily that the gentleman himself did not much care for the *ton* and their gossip.

"I quite understand," Emily replied, kindly. "But you need not worry for my sake, Lord Henderson. I have experienced a good deal since I first returned to London and believe that I can deal with such comments, whispers and looks as regards my presence here."

Lord Henderson heaved a long sigh but then smiled at her. "The rumor mill is constantly at work, is it not?" he stated, spreading his arm wide. "Now, to whom might I escort you?"

Emily felt the sudden sensation of dozens of pairs of eyes turning to look at her and felt a knot forming in her stomach. She lifted her chin and surveyed the scene before her with apparent calmness, ignoring the tightness that ran through her.

And then, she saw him.

Her breath shuddered out of her as Lord Havisham began to make his way towards her, his intentions clear. Emily began to look desperately amongst the crowd, seeking someone else she might speak to, but it was much too late. Lord Havisham had already arrived and was now bowing in front of them both. Behind him, the assembled group of guests turned back to each other, their conversations picking up in both speed and volume all over again.

"Lord Havisham," Lord Henderson said, cheerfully. "I quite forgot that you are already acquainted with Lady Smithton." A sound caught his attention and he twisted his head over his shoulder, a smile brightening his expression. "Ah, I see that Lady Cecelia has arrived, along with her mother." He turned back to Emily and gave her a broad grin. "Do excuse me, Lady Smithton. I shall leave you with Lord Havisham, whom I am certain will ensure you have something to drink very soon." This was said with a pointed glance in Lord Havisham's direction, who merely nodded and smiled.

Emily's heart turned over in her chest.

"I do not feel particularly thirsty," she said, as though this would be reason enough to leave him behind as she sought out another acquaintance. "You need not accompany me, Lord Havisham."

"But I wish to." He moved to stand beside her, so that they might move through the crowd together, leaving Emily feeling trapped and uncertain. "I know what you said the last time we spoke, Lady Smithton, but you did not give me the time to reply." His eyes crinkled at the corners as he inclined his head. "For my part, I do not have any desire to separate from you in the way you suggested, nor do I see any need for our acquaintance to end." Clearing his throat, he lifted his head again, as though in saying such a thing, their friendship could then simply continue as it had done before. "I do hope you have had an enjoyable few days, Lady Smithton, since I last saw you."

A slight sheen of sweat broke out on Emily's forehead. She had thought that Lord Havisham would be content to end their acquaintance but now, it seemed, he was not inclined to do so. His ease of manner and his jovial questions suggested that he sought to begin their friendship anew, in the hope that she might forgive him for his past failings and accept his apologies. Could she truly do so? Emily knew that in order to truly set her face to the future and to turn her back on all that had gone before, she would need to find a way to make her peace with what Lord Havisham had done, and yet every time she thought of his rejection, the pain still stung at her heart. She wanted to be free of him, wanted to feel nothing, but her heart would not allow her to do so. Sighing inwardly, she looked up at him and decided that she could, at the very least, be amenable.

"I have been vastly busy," she told him, moving slowly forward. "I have two new acquaintances who called upon me, so that I might get to know them better."

Lord Havisham frowned, his lips pulling into a thin line. "Is that so?" he muttered, his displeasure evident at once. "I am surprised to hear it, Lady Smithton."

Emily opened her mouth in order to give him a sharp retort, but something held her back. Glancing up at Lord Havisham, she saw that his expression was dark, his eyes darting from place to place. Evidently, he believed that these 'acquaintances' were gentlemen, which obviously brought him a good deal of frustration – and Emily found herself having no eagerness to remove that suggestion from him.

"Why should you be surprised?" she asked, innocently. "I have discovered that the number of my acquaintances has steadily increased since I have returned to London and that can be no bad thing."

Lord Havisham said nothing for a moment or two, before he cleared his throat and put a smile on his face – a smile which, Emily noticed, did not reach his eyes.

"Of course," he replied, with an easiness of manner that Emily knew to be a pretense. "I am glad that you find yourself in better circumstances, Lady Smithton."

She glanced up at him, allowing a coy smile to tip her lips. "You said that you found me changed, Lord

Havisham, in my manner of speaking and in my determination. I do hope that you think that such a change has been a good thing?"

Lord Havisham looked at her in surprise. "Of course I do, Lady Smithton," he replied, with a fervency she had not expected. "You cannot know just how much joy it brings me to see you as free as you are now. I recall how you were when your father was a dark shadow behind you and how difficult such a circumstance was for you."

Emily stopped, taking a glass from the nearby footman's tray, and turning sharp eyes onto Lord Havisham. "You could see my struggle."

"You are well aware that I saw it all," he replied, gently. "I will not pretend otherwise, Lady Smithton. But, as I said, I am relieved to see you free of it now. You have blossomed into a delightful flower that has, thus far, hidden its petals from the sun."

This compliment brought a slight pink to Emily's lips, but she did not allow herself to be overcome by it. "I discovered the beginnings of my strength the day you turned from me, Lord Havisham," she told him, candidly. "I realized that if none were able to come to my aid – for even my mother could do nothing to help me – then I had to find the courage and determination needed to make my life as bearable as it could be." She saw Lord Havisham about to speak but held up one hand, so as to silence him. "My husband was neither a kind nor a good man. Instead, he was nothing but cruel and demanding, just as my father was. The way he chose to torment me, with harsh truths and mocking words tore at my spirits, but it did not break me entirely." Taking in a steadying breath and silently wondering why she was suddenly so eager to share all of this with Lord Havisham, Emily could not stop herself from continuing. "Lord Smithton was old and rotund. His threats of physical consequences should I refuse him came to naught and I slowly began to realize that I had the capacity to turn from his requests."

"And so, your courage began to grow within you."

She nodded, looking into Lord Havisham's eyes and seeing compassion lingering there. For a moment, she wanted to throw herself into his arms, wanted to melt into his embrace and feel herself in the only place she had ever wanted to be – but then she steadied herself and turned her head away. "I began to transform, Lord Havisham. His death only spurred that. I shall not pretend to grieve over the loss of him, as I have stated to many others. I did not care for him. In fact, I found myself retreating from him whenever I could." Another sigh rippled from her lips. "And since that moment, I have discovered a life where I am obligated to no-one other than to myself."

Lord Havisham said nothing for a few minutes, silence lingering between them. All around Emily came the sound of conversation and laughter from the other guests, but she paid them no heed. Instead, all she saw was the look in Lord Havisham's blue eyes, the slight wrinkle to his forehead that spoke of concern and relief at the same time. Did he think her unknown to him now? Or was he truly pleased that she had become someone entirely new?

"I can see that you have no need of me any longer, Lady Smithton."

Surprised, she stared up into his face.

"That is," he stammered, suddenly appearing quite uncomfortable. "That is, I am aware that you do not need me any longer, in the way you once did."

Blinking rapidly, Emily tried to keep her outward composure, even though her thoughts were running furiously through her mind. "I do not understand completely what you mean, Lord Havisham."

He sighed and ran one hand lightly over his fair hair. "What I mean to say, Lady Smithton, is that you have no need of my company in the same way as you once did." His eyes lingered on her face, running over her eyes, her lips, her cheeks. "I knew in my heart that there was something of importance growing between us but I turned from it instead of pursuing it. I will admit that I was, mayhap, a little flattered with the way that you sought me."

A flush of mortification crept up Emily's face and she turned her head away.

"I confess my selfishness and my arrogance to you, Lady Smithton," Lord Havisham continued, without pausing. "But I will not pretend that the affection in my heart for you was not genuine, nor will I lie and say that it has gone from me. For I can assure you that it has not done so."

Emily caught her breath but did not lift her eyes to his face, keeping her gaze steadfastly towards the other side of the room.

"You do not know what to say, I think, Lady Smithton," Lord Havisham finished, heavily, his shoulders slumping as she shot him a quick glance. "Yet again, I make my foolishness apparent to you but I will not regret it, not this time."

"It is as I have said," Emily replied, tightly, turning her head to look back at him directly, aware of how quickly her heart was beating. "We need not be in each other's company, Lord Havisham. You sought me out this evening and I – "

Lord Havisham held up a hand, shaking his head as he interrupted her. "No, Lady Smithton," he said, gently. "The last thing I wish for is for there to be an end to what has been between us. That is not at all what I intend. You have misunderstood everything about my determination to speak to you, I fear."

"Misunderstand you?" she repeated, a look of confusion in her expression. "Whatever do you mean, Lord Havisham?"

Her astonishment increased all the more as he took a step closer, his expression gentling. She could feel his breath on her cheek as she looked up at him. His fingers sought hers again, grasping them surreptitiously so that no other guest would see. Lead poured into her limbs, fixing her in position as shock ran straight through her.

"My dear Lady Smithton," Lord Havisham murmured quietly, taking another small step closer so that he might look even more deeply into her eyes. "I cannot allow this to be the end of our acquaintance. I cannot bear it. Please, do not force it upon me. My heart has never forgotten you and even though I have behaved in the most appalling and upsetting manner, I shall do all I can to show you that I am no longer that faint-hearted gentleman you once knew. I would not seek to allow this acquaintance to die, Lady Smithton. Pray, say that you can give me even a modicum of hope in my ventures." His eyes searched her face, but Emily's expression remained tight. "If you say that you cannot forgive me, however, if you say that you cannot turn to me as you once did, then I shall not force my wishes upon you. It is only that I could not allow this moment to pass without being clear with you about what I intend."

Emily swallowed, her heart in her throat. "Then what is it you intend, Lord Havisham?" she asked, trying to fill her voice with lightness but failing completely. Her anxiety was great, her mind telling her to step away from him but her heart forcing her to stay, her fingers still caught in his.

Lord Havisham lowered his head so as to speak only to her, his thumb running over the back of her hand. "I intend to try and win your affections again so that I might do what I should have done all those years ago."

CHAPTER TEN

"You have another gift, my lady."

Emily closed her eyes tightly as Lord Havisham's sixth bunch of roses appeared in a vase in front of her.

"And the note with it, my lady."

She did not know what to say to him, aware that her usually stoic butler now had a small glint of delight in his eyes.

"Take this one to my bedchamber," she said on a whim. "If I am to receive so many roses, then I may best make use of them! My whole house shall smell beautiful."

The butler smiled and picked up the vase again. "Of course, my lady. Do you require anything else?"

She shook her head, wanting some quiet with which to think. "Not at the moment."

"Very good, my lady."

The door closed tightly and Emily was returned to the peace and quiet she had been enjoying before the appearance of yet another bunch of flowers. She looked down at the note in her hand, feeling butterflies fill her stomach. Lord Havisham had sent her a bunch of flowers and a note every day since he had spoken so openly to her in the middle of Lord Henderson's soiree. She had been so astonished by his declaration to win her affections again that she had stared at him for a few moments not knowing what to say to such a statement. Part of her had cried aloud with the delight and the promise that was contained in such words, whilst another part of her rebelled against him, not wanting to allow herself to even give credence to such an offer, for fear of what it would do to her. Instead, she had simply looked up at him in silence before turning on her heel and moving to another part of the room, placing a broad smile on her face to cover the shock that ran through her. Lord Havisham had let her go, clearly aware that what he had said had stunned her. He had not sought her out for the rest of the evening and since that time, had not made any attempt to draw near her again, even though they had been in company together. There was a wariness in Emily's heart when it came to Lord Havisham. She did not know what it was she felt nor what it was she wanted. It was as though her determination to live a life of freedom, unattached and independent, had suddenly been shaken so fiercely that she did not know what to do with herself any longer.

Sighing, she closed her eyes for a moment before looking down at the note in her hand. Lord Havisham had written much the same words to her these last six days, so she knew very well what would be within. All the same, Emily could not bring herself to set it aside. If she was honest with herself, she wanted to read the words that were within, wanted to see what would be said this time. A little irritated with her own weakness, she turned the note over and broke the seal, flattening it out carefully.

Her eyes scanned the page, taking in Lord Havisham's words. He had an excellent hand but it was the tenderness that was expressed that caught her heart.

"'I have done you a great wrong, Emily. Allow me to make amends, I pray you. One final chance is all I seek. Tell me that you have not forgotten me in the same way that I have not forgotten you.'"

As much as she disliked it, tears filled her eyes. There were feelings deep within her that had never been resolved, feelings that she did not want to even consider anymore. However, the fact that Lord Havisham insisted on not only sending her gifts but writing to her also on a daily basis, meant that she was forced to consider them more and more. If she were to let him back into her life, if she were to let him court her, then that would mean those feelings might return in all their intensity and she was not certain that this was something she wanted. Had she not already convinced herself that she did not wish to marry? That she did not want to let anyone make her so vulnerable again?

And yet there was something that drew her to him, no matter how hard she fought it.

What am I to do?

Putting the note aside, Emily let the face of Lord Havisham linger in her mind a little longer. There had once been that intimacy between them that she knew could easily be rekindled, but that would mean a true forgetting of their past and a willingness to trust him once again. She could not easily do that, she knew, not when her trust in him had already been shattered. But could it be something that she could, at the very least, allow herself to consider?

Emily bit her lip, passing a hand over her eyes as she blinked her tears away. She would not cry over Lord Havisham again, not when she had done so before and for far too long. She had to look at this matter with sober judgment, had to allow herself to consider everything with clear rationality. The only problem with such a consideration was that her heart did not allow herself to think clearly, for it swarmed with such feelings that she could barely make sense of them. To be free to live as she pleased and to do as she wished was what she had always dreamt of, was it not? And it was a life that she had only just begun to enjoy, for finally, the gossip about her late husband and her part in it had begun to fade.

Lord Havisham will not seek to remove that freedom from you, Emily.

The quiet voice in her head made Emily hesitate, closing her eyes tightly at the swarm of thoughts that ran through her. She knew that Lord Havisham was not the sort of gentleman who would demand anything of her. He would respect her, consider her and care for her, if she would allow him. Had he not spoken of his affection for her? The feelings within his heart that had not faded away but, in her absence, only grown stronger. Emily knew that she could not compare Lord Havisham with either her late husband or her father. He had made a mistake, he had said, in allowing her to marry Lord Smithton instead of securing her for his wife but had realized it much too late. That had caused him no end of regret but she had been the one who had needed to marry Lord Smithton regardless.

But if you had not married Lord Smithton, then you would not have found this strength of character that now fills you with both courage and determination.

Having been forced to marry Lord Smithton was not something Emily would ever be grateful for but she could not pretend that finding her confidence and strength had not been of some blessing. If she could see goodness in her past circumstances, then could she not set aside all the frustration and the pain that sometimes still stung at her when she thought of Lord Havisham, so that she might consider her future?

A long sigh left her lips, her head feeling heavy and weighted with all that she felt. "And I shall not think of him now," she told herself, folding up the note and placing it with the others. "For there is much now to prepare."

Deciding to host a dinner party had either been a very wise or a very foolish idea. Emily could not yet decide which it was for, as she looked around the table, she saw some eyes looking back at her with interest, whilst others seemed more delighted in the company that was present. It was, Emily considered, as she finished her dessert, rather unfortunate that even still, there were those amongst the *beau monde* who wished for nothing more than to feed on gossip and rumor. To have been invited to attend Lady Smithton's dinner would be a notable event indeed and she was quite certain that one or two of her guests would waste no time in telling all of their acquaintances about it. Thankfully, those whispers had died down a good deal over the last few days, since there were more than enough scandals for the *beau monde* to feed on. She was, it seemed, now a good deal less interesting than she had been before.

Smiling to herself, Emily allowed her gaze to run across the table. Miss Bavidge and Miss Crosby were present, with both sitting quietly in their seats, their spoons down on the table having already finished their dessert. A flicker of a frown crossed Emily's expression, seeing them sitting without any attempt at conversation. She had made sure to invite a good few gentlemen that she knew to be of good reputation, although some were inclined to be something of a rogue at times, but she had thought that to be of benefit to her two friends. They would have to learn how to manage a gentleman's less than proper behavior, particularly if one attempted to flirt outrageously. However, such a thing was not about to occur given that neither of them seemed to be making any attempt to engage with those about them.

Frustrated that she had not kept a closer eye on them both during the previous courses, Emily set her spoon down and tried to think of what she could say that would force either Miss Bavidge or Miss Crosby to speak. At least they both looked well enough, although she would

have to make the suggestion that Miss Crosby do something with the ringlets that always seemed to be hanging
down on either side of her face. They gave her a heaviness that did not suit her.

"Might we leave the gentlemen to their port?" she
murmured, seeing that her guests were finished. "Ladies,
there will be tea set out for us in the drawing room." She
rose gracefully and gave the gentlemen a lingering smile.
"Do take as long as you wish."

Grateful for the opportunity to grasp Miss Bavidge's
arm and catch Miss Crosby's eye, Emily waited until the
three of them were ensconced together in a quiet part of
the drawing room. Tea had already been served and the
ladies were talking quietly amongst themselves, with
some eagerly awaiting the reappearance of the
gentlemen.

"You have been very quiet this evening, Miss
Bavidge," Emily began, looking towards Miss Crosby. "As
have you, Miss Crosby. What is it that keeps you so
silent?"

Miss Bavidge blushed furiously, her eyes lowering to
her lap. "I fear that I have become rather afraid of
speaking aloud, for fear that someone will make some
comment about my father," she replied, honestly.

"And I am not particularly interesting," Miss Crosby
replied, with such calm certainty that Emily found
herself rather taken aback. "I might fade into the
shadows and no-one would recall that I have ever been
present."

Emily did not know what to say to this, hearing no
hint of sadness in Miss Crosby's tone but rather a sense of

acceptance, as though she truly believed this to be the case.

"I do not think that can be true," she managed to say, her mind whirling. "I know that at least one gentleman cast his eyes over you this evening."

This seemed to dumbfound Miss Crosby, for her eyes widened and she stared blankly back at Emily as though she could not quite believe it.

"And Viscount Morton asked you one or two questions, did he not?" Emily asked, turning her attention back to Miss Bavidge, who now looked up with a small look of hope in her eyes. "Did you not respond to him?"

"I did," Miss Bavidge replied, quickly, "but it was about nothing in particular. Although," she continued, her cheeks still a little red, "I should be grateful that he did not ask about my father."

Emily smiled and nodded. "Indeed," she replied, wondering if she was being encouraging in any way at all, or if she was failing miserably. "You must be a little more assertive. That is the only way you will be noticed."

The two young ladies exchanged glances but both nodded their assent. Emily smiled and made to say more, only for the door to open and the gentlemen to walk through.

Gentlemen who included Lord Havisham, Emily noted with astonishment. She had not invited him for dinner, so what could he be doing here at this moment?

Lord Havisham must have seen her astonishment, for he came over to her at once and inclined his head.

"I am sorry to have intruded so," he said, quickly, bowing in front of her. "It is only that I have heard some news that I thought important to share with you, Lady Smithton." His eyes roved towards Miss Bavidge and Miss Crosby, who both attempted to look as though they were not at all interested in what he had to say.

Emily tipped her head up to look into Lord Havisham's eyes, aware of how quickly her heart had trembled with delight upon seeing him. "What news is this, Lord Havisham?" she asked, rising quickly and finding herself a little anxious given the serious look in his eyes. "Has something occurred?"

Lord Havisham hesitated, then turned around so that his back was to Miss Bavidge and Miss Crosby.

"It is only that I have heard your father has returned to town, Lady Smithton," he said, making Emily's breath hitch with shock. "Your mother is with him also."

Emily swayed suddenly, not quite certain what to make of this. "My father," she repeated, trying to force herself to believe it. "I have not seen him since the day I wed." Not that he had not attempted to force himself back into her life after the death of her husband, telling her that she needed to return to his household and, of course, do his bidding as she had done before.

"I do not know why he is in town," Lord Havisham said, looking at her as though he feared she might faint with the shock of it. "But I thought it best you know at once."

Swallowing hard, Emily took in a long breath and tried to smile. "The rumors about my husband's death came from my father, I am quite certain of it."

Lord Havisham frowned. "But why should he do such a thing?"

She let out a wry laugh, her face contorted with pain. "You know how much he liked to find fault with me, do you not? When I would not go back to his house, when I would not do as he asked, then the rumors began. I fear he has come to London to try and persuade me to return to his household. No doubt so that he can force me to wed another gentleman in order to make some profit for himself." She shook her head and closed her eyes momentarily, feeling herself swaying slightly. "I shall not do as he asks."

"No, you shall not," Lord Havisham replied, fervently. "I have seen your strength and determination, Lady Smithton. You need not fear him and, should you require it, I shall be by your side ready to stand against your father's demands."

She smiled at him, the shock draining from her. "That is very much appreciated, Lord Havisham," she replied, quietly, touched by not only his offer of support but his concern for her. He had come to speak to her directly upon discovering that her father had returned to London, so that she would not be caught unawares. That spoke of a genuine consideration for her, which warmed her heart and brought a smile to her lips.

"You know that I would not allow you to be without friends, Lady Smithton," he murmured, taking a step away from her and inclining his head. "Thank you for allowing me to speak to you. I shall depart now."

"Wait."

The word was out of her mouth before she could prevent. Lord Havisham turned slowly, his expression hopeful.

"You are more than welcome to stay for a short time, Lord Havisham," Emily stammered, suddenly feeling a little embarrassed. "If you wish to, that is."

It was as though she had offered him something wonderful, for his eyes lit up and a broad smile tugged his lips wide. "I should be delighted to stay, Lady Smithton," he replied, with a quick bow. "I thank you."

"You are very welcome," she replied, with as much dignity as she could manage. "And thank you for your consideration, Lord Havisham. I am grateful for the urgency with which you have informed me of my father's return to London."

His smile softened, his eyes growing tender. "You are always in my thoughts, Lady Smithton," he replied, in such a low voice that she had to strain to hear him. "I am glad to have been able to aid you in this."

Emily could find nothing to say, her throat constricting as she held his gaze. It was only when he turned away that she realized she had been holding her breath, one hand pressed against her stomach as she felt her heart tug towards him with a renewed determination.

It seemed she was going to be able to forgive him after all.

CHAPTER ELEVEN

"*Y*ou have a visitor, Lady Smithton."

Emily drew in a long breath as she took the card from the butler. It bore her father's name and, as such, gave her such a feeling of tension that she had to grasp the back of the chair with a tight hand.

"Is my mother with him?" she asked, as the butler waited patiently in front of her. "Or does he come alone?"

The butler responded at once. "Alone, my lady. Do you wish to see him or should I ask him to call another time?"

Emily hesitated. Her immediate response was to ask the butler to send her father from the house, for she certainly did not want to see him. However, that would mean she was giving into her fear and her fright, reducing herself to the quiet little mouse she had once been. No, if she was to deal with her father, then she would have to show him that she was both independent and unafraid.

He would not have the same hold on her as he had done before.

"No, I shall see him," she said, suddenly, before she had time to change her mind. "Do send for tea and refreshments also."

The butler nodded and withdrew, giving Emily some time to think about what she would say once she had seen her father. Most likely, he would demand that she do as he ask, now that she was widowed, but Emily had no intention of returning to his household. Her father had sold her once and she was not about to give him the opportunity to do so again.

The door opened and Emily turned to face it, drawing herself up to her full height and clasping her hands loosely in front of her. Her father stormed in, his face dark and his eyes malevolent.

"Emily," he grated, without waiting for her to speak. "How dare you behave in such a fashion?"

Emily held her breath, looking at her father and being reminded of just how often he had attempted to shame her with his angry exclamations. Letting it out slowly, she looked at him with as much calmness in her expression as she could muster. "Good afternoon, father," she began, gesturing for him to sit down. "What an unexpected visit this is. Might I inquire as to your health?"

Lord Chesterton glared at her, his eyes narrowing. "You are being impertinent, Emily. I ask you again, how dare you behave in such a fashion as this? Going about London as though you have no consideration for the gossip and rumor that is being pushed through the streets about you!"

Emily, thinking that since her father would not sit down, she may as well do so, took a seat carefully and tried to consider what she should say in response. The knowledge that she had no requirement to do as her father asked brought her a great sense of relief, allowing her to breathe at a fairly normal rate. She let the silence grow between them, looking at her father and seeing his face begin to darken. She would not allow herself to be afraid of him again, not when she had nothing to fear. He could not come near her. He could not demand that she obey him. There was nothing between them now.

"It is rather tiresome, I will admit," she said, softly, looking up into his face and finding her hands tighten in her lap at the sight of the rage in his expression. "The rumors are nothing more than that, however, and I will not permit them to keep me back from society."

"Not even if they are true?"

His words bounced off the walls, making Emily lift an eyebrow. "But they are not true, father, as I am certain you must believe," she replied, a twist to her gut reminding her that, most likely, the whispers about her behavior had come from him in an attempt to have her return to his household with the shame and sorrow of it all. "I am, therefore, ignoring them entirely."

"That will not do!" her father exclaimed, beginning to pace back and forth in front of her. "You are behaving irrationally, Emily. You ought to be keeping to the shadows and not pushing yourself forward in amongst society. In fact," he continued, his voice still overly loud as he turned to look at her. "You should return home, as I have suggested."

Emily's hands tightened together at once, her lips thinning as she watched him pace. She had known that this was his intention and yet the pain of his disregard for her bit at her all over again.

"Whom is it you have promised me to this time, father?" she asked, sharply, arching one eyebrow as he stopped pacing and turned to look at her. "You need not pretend that you have not done so, for I am well aware that the only reason you are urging me home is to set me up as wife for someone else." This had never been confirmed by either Emily's mother or father but she did not need to hear the words from their mouth to know that this was the truth. The arrested look on her father's face proclaimed that she had been quite correct in believing this to be his goal. A long sigh escaped her lips as she shook her head in his direction, her sadness weighing down her soul for some moments. Why did he care nothing for her? Why was his only consideration the wealth that he could gain from her marriage to a gentleman of his choosing?

"You are a repugnant little brat!"

Emily flinched and drew back sharply as Lord Chesterton suddenly threw himself forward, one hand raised to slap her. She closed her eyes, cringing, her hands tight on the chair arms as she waited, only for another, authoritative voice to ring across the room.

"I do not think that is wise, Chesterton."

Her eyes flaring with surprise whilst her heart flooded with relief, Emily looked behind her father's frozen stance to see none other than Lord Havisham walk into the room. His eyes were darker than she had ever seen them, his brows low and his hands planted firmly on his hips.

"H- Havisham, is it not?" Lord Chesterton said, making no move to step away from Emily. "This is none of your business, sir." He turned back to Emily, his face a deep shade of red, only for Lord Havisham to stride forward and grasp Lord Chesterton's arm, thrusting it hard behind his back. Lord Chesterton let out a howl of pain and staggered away, leaving Emily free to rise from her chair now that her father was no longer standing directly in front of her.

"It may be so that this conversation has nothing whatsoever to do with me," Lord Havisham stated, coming to stand between Emily and her father. "But I shall not permit you to harm Lady Smithton in any way."

Emily swallowed hard but took a small step to her right, so that she might see her father completely. "And I will not do as you ask, father," she stated, clearly, despite the fear curling in her belly. "I have lived that life and I need live it no longer. I am a widow of independent means. I have no need to live by your requirements any longer." Her voice grew louder as her determination grew. "I may have once been the mouse, easily enough directed where to go, but those days are long gone from my mind now. You have no business demanding what I should do, father."

Her father shook a pointed finger at her. "You have made an excellent match, have you not?"

"Only for Lord Smithton to pay you for me!" she exclaimed, hearing the expulsion of air that came from her father's lips as she told him what she knew. "And now you would wish me to do the same as I have done before and subjugate myself to another, so that you may find a little more money from the sale." Her anger began to burn, her fear fading away. "You care nothing for me, father. You have never done so. All you see is the money you could make from me."

"And that is why you started the rumors," Lord Havisham added, with a quick look of sympathy in Emily's direction. "You wanted Emily to be so shamed that she would return to you – and you would then treat her as you had done before and marry her off to whomever you chose. For a good deal of coin, I would suggest."

Lord Chesterton's eyes narrowed as he glared at Lord Havisham. "You have no say in this, Lord Havisham!" he declared. "Might I suggest that you depart this house –"

"Whilst you may think that you have some say in my life, father," Emily interrupted, loudly, coming to stand a little closer to Lord Havisham, "I can assure you that you have no right to demand that Lord Havisham quit my house. It is not the case. *I* wish for Lord Havisham to remain and so he shall." Lifting her chin and finding a good deal of courage within her heart as she glanced up at Lord Havisham, Emily prepared to speak what she hoped would be her final words to her father. She did not want to see him again, did not want to have him interrupt her life in any way. He had to understand that she would never again do as he urged.

"Father," she began, taking a step closer to him and seeing the way that his eyes turned back to her, their dark orbs threatening and malevolent. "I am not the girl you once knew. I shall not return to your house, nor shall I ever again acquiesce to your demands." She held herself steady, her shoulders firm and her eyes lifted to his without fear nor anxiety within her. "I have done as you bade me once before and yet, despite the troubles I have faced, I have discovered myself to be courageous and strong. I am able to do as I wish now, able to behave as I choose. I shall never again be the child you believed me to be, the one who had no choice but to do as you bade her for fear of the consequences that would follow if she did not. You do not know me any longer, father, and I have no desire to allow you that opportunity." She drew in a long breath, seeing her father about to speak and held up one hand in a sharp, deft motion that had her father gasping with the shock of her audacity. "Now, you will quit my house, father, and return to your own abode. If you do not, then you shall find yourself physically removed by my footmen. And have no doubt of this: you shall never be welcomed in my presence or even in this house again."

She did not wait to see how he responded but instead turned on her heel and walked to the window. Her stomach tightened as silence washed over the room, closing her eyes as she prayed that her father would do as she had bidden him. Much to her relief, some moments later, the sound of his footsteps reached her ears. The door was pulled open and his footsteps began to fade as it closed tightly behind him.

"He is gone."

Lord Havisham was beside her in a moment, his hand resting on her shoulder. Emily put her hand up to his, feeling both relief and fondness filling her.

"Thank you for your support in this, Lord Havisham," she murmured, too afraid to look up into his face for what she feared would follow. "Never have I been so glad to see your face."

"I am glad to hear it, Lady Smithton," came the gentle reply. "If it is not too bold to say, I am truly proud of your conduct towards your father. You were gracious yet determined and it is your courage that has forced him to obey your requests. I do not think that you need fear him again."

Emily sighed and dared to look up into Lord Havisham's face, seeing the affection in his eyes and finding herself lost within them. "I am glad of that," she admitted, softly. "And I am glad to find you here now, Lord Havisham."

A beat passed before Lord Havisham responded. It was as though her words had been too much for him to immediately accept.

"Does this mean, my dear Lady Smithton, that you have forgiven me my past misdemeanors?"

She nodded, a smile spreading across her face as Lord Havisham closed his eyes and let out a breath of relief. "It does, Lord Havisham," she told him, feeling the wounds in her heart finally healing completely. "I have forgiven you completely. There is nothing else that needs to be said."

CHAPTER TWELVE

"What am I to do with them?"

It was the day after Emily's father had marched into the house and demanded that she return to his household. The day after Lord Havisham had stood by her as she had spoken to her father, and since she had finally told Lord Havisham that there was nothing left for her to forgive. The freedom that came with such a thing had been quite overwhelming and even though no more had been said between them, Emily knew that the possibilities were now fully open to her. She did not need to decide immediately what she would do about the future as regarded Lord Havisham but would rather enjoy the happiness and the joy that now came with setting the past aside. Now, they would be able to start to rebuild their acquaintance.

However, Emily did not want to forget about Miss Bavidge and Miss Crosby. Whilst she wished to aid them, she found it more than difficult to think of what she might do in order to encourage them to engage with any gentlemen that came to greet them. She did not know how to teach them what to do when it came to a gentleman's flirtations.

And then, an idea caught her. Rising to her feet, she began to pace excitedly about the room, realizing that this might be the perfect way to align both of the difficulties in her life – the two ladies, Miss Bavidge and Miss Crosby – and the other being Lord Havisham. If she were to manage this correctly, then not only could she do her best to find happiness for Miss Bavidge and Miss Crosby, but it would also give herself the opportunity to get to know Lord Havisham all over again without truly committing herself to anything more than a furthering of their acquaintance.

Clapping her hands in delight, Emily rang the bell at once, hurrying to her writing desk. She had three notes to write in very quick succession and the staff would need to know to expect three guests for late afternoon tea. She could hardly wait to see them.

A few hours later and Emily rose to her feet as the butler opened the door to her guests. However, it was not only Miss Bavidge and Miss Crosby who appeared but, instead, they entered with two other ladies alongside them. Miss Bavidge, who was blushing furiously and worrying her lip, curtsied beautifully before clearing her throat to speak.

"I was just about to write a note to you when I received your summons," she said, her voice rather timid. "I am terribly sorry to be so rude all over again but I have two further acquaintances who wished to know you and to see if they might, perhaps, join our little endeavour."

Emily shook her head, her lips quirking as she looked at them all, seeing four rather scared looking young ladies all glancing at one another nervously. So, she had gone from two young ladies to four – but what did that matter? It would only mean that there might be a little more work to do on her part and it could certainly take a little more time to aid them all, but that was of no concern to her. She herself had no eagerness to rush into any kind of courtship with Lord Havisham and this would bring her the time she needed.

"Indeed, I can see that you have brought some friends with you, Miss Bavidge," she murmured, allowing a small smile onto her face as she turned to greet the two ladies whom she believed to be ages with Miss Bavidge. Both were just coming out of a deep curtsy. "And do you both consider yourselves spinsters too?"

There was one young lady with very dark hair and piercing green eyes who, at first glance, appeared to be something of a beauty but it was only when she moved forward to curtsy that Emily noticed she limped just a little. Her heart swelled with sympathy. The *ton* did not take kindly to imperfections.

"Lady Amelia Ferguson, daughter to the late Earl of Stockbridge," she murmured, her head still low as the second lady came forward. She was not hiding her face as the other did but looked directly at Emily before curtsying again, as if to make up for her rudeness in appearing without invitation. She was neither plain nor pretty, with mousey brown hair and warm hazel eyes that seemed to take everything in.

"Lady Beatrice Thornton," she said, stepping back. "My father is the Marquess of Burnley."

"And, as I asked, you both consider yourself spinsters?" Emily asked, a little uncertain as to why Lady Beatrice would be so, given that she was the daughter of a marquess.

Lady Beatrice nodded, as did Lady Amelia. "My father has recently declared to his fellow gentlemen, under the influence of a good deal of liquor, that my mother played him false before she carried me. There is now some question over my lineage and thus, I am rejected."

Emily shook her head, indicating for them all be seated. "How terrible. I am sorry, Lady Beatrice."

Lady Beatrice nodded but looked away, clearly battling to remain perfectly in control. Emily could not help but feel sympathy for her – for them all.

"You do not mind, Lady Smithton?" Miss Bavidge whispered, still looking terrified that they might all be suddenly thrown from her house. "I am sorry to have done so without your knowledge but – "

Emily waved a hand, cutting her off. "No, not in the least. Four ladies is a perfect size for 'The Spinsters Guild'."

Four pairs of eyes looked back at her in astonishment and Emily could not help but laugh.

"That is what we shall call this little endeavour," she explained, as they all looked back at her wordlessly. "To anyone who asks, we simply meet to sew and discuss and the like. Those who are betrothed or already wed are not a part of our circle and I shall make it quite clear that you have all been carefully chosen." She tilted her head and smiled. "But, of course, we shall, in actuality, be discussing your futures and I shall help you where I can. I am sure that, by the time this Season ends, you shall all find yourselves in a much happier situation. And, if you do not, then I shall simply return next Season to do the same!"

There was a short, stunned silence as the four ladies looked back at her, their expressions all ones of surprise.

"Thank you, Lady Smithton," Miss Crosby whispered, blinking back a sudden flurry of tears. "You have brought hope back into my heart."

Emily smiled at her gently. "You will not be alone any longer, my dear. You have my word that I will do all I can to help you."

The room was then filled with the sound of the three other ladies thanking Emily profusely and Emily felt her heart grow warm as she looked at them all. This was working out wonderfully.

"Oh," she said, interrupting them as there came a scratch at the door. "Do excuse me for a moment. I have another guest that I must speak to in private, although he is to aid us in this."

Silence filled the room.

"A – a gentleman?" Lady Beatrice enquired, carefully. "A gentleman is to assist us?"

A smile tugged at Emily's lips. "He does not know it yet but yes, he will assist us all. After all, we will need a gentleman to show an initial interest in you, to dance with you and the like and I am quite sure that Lord Havisham is up to the task." Walking to the door, she opened it and saw the butler waiting outside. "Do excuse me for a few minutes."

There was a knot in her stomach as Emily opened the door and walked into the parlor to see Lord Havisham waiting for her. He was standing with his back to her, his hands clasped loosely behind his back as he looked out of the window onto the London street below.

"Lord Havisham," she began, as he turned towards her. "Thank you for coming."

He remained exactly where he was, although his eyes, so blue and intense, fixed on her own and a gentle tug of his lips told her that he was truly delighted to see her. "I would do anything you wish, Lady Smithton."

That brought a smile to her face. "I am glad to hear it; Lord Havisham for I have a proposal for you. Please, be seated."

A look of curiosity on his face, he did as she asked and sat down carefully, his hands resting loosely on the arms of the chair. Emily felt herself grow a little nervous as she spoke, wondering what he would think of it all.

"Lord Havisham, you have made it very clear that you intend to try and win back my heart. After yesterday's meeting with my father and my decision to forgive all that has gone before, I must tell you that I have given the matter a great deal of consideration."

Heat flared in his eyes. "And what have you decided, Lady Smithton?"

Pausing, she looked at him directly. "I have decided that I cannot accept your offer to court me as yet, Lord Havisham."

He crumpled almost at once, his shoulders slumping as he sank back into his chair. The look of disappointment in his expression caught at her heart for a moment, but she dismissed it outright. This was perfectly fair on her part, for trust took time to rebuild.

"Lord Havisham, I do not yet know how to trust you," she said quietly. "The deep friendship and intimacy that was there before has gone entirely, although I will not pretend that my heart is without any affection." She hesitated for a moment before continuing. "However –"

Lord Havisham's head shot up; his eyes filled with a sudden, fierce hope.

"However," she continued, her fingers tightening together as she held her hands in her lap. "I have only just begun an endeavour that I could use your help with. It may take some time to complete but that would give us the time required to reacquaint ourselves with one another. It would also give me the opportunity to study my own heart and to consider the feelings that dwell within it."

It did not surprise her that Lord Havisham began to nod fervently, clearly more than willing to do whatever it was she asked. That in itself brought a small smile to her face.

"What say you, Lord Havisham?" she asked gently. "Are you willing to aid me in this?"

"Of course I am!" he exclaimed, sitting forward in his seat with such earnestness on his face that she was forced to hide her smile. "I can only thank you for such a consideration, Lady Smithton, for I well understand that what I did was almost entirely unforgivable. You cannot know the joy that this has brought me." He took a breath, closing his eyes so as to calm himself somewhat. "I would welcome the chance to prove that my heart is still true to you, Lady Smithton. To show you that I have thought of no other and that my only desire is to have you as my own."

Emily nodded slowly, her heart picking up its pace just a little as her eyes caught his, seeing how they almost glowed with an earnest affection.

"Very well, Lord Havisham," she said, softly. "I thank you for your willingness in this. I suppose then, that it is time to introduce you to the others." Rising from her chair, she waited for him to do the same, finding the confused expression on his face to be a little humorous.

"The others?" he asked, slowly getting to his feet. "I did not understand that this endeavour of yours involved any other persons."

Walking to the door, she walked through and back towards the drawing room, with Lord Havisham following closely behind. Coming to a stop just at the door, she placed one hand on the door handle and looked up into his face. He was looking down at her with confusion written into every line of his expression, his brows knotting as she smiled at him.

"Lord Havisham," she said, in a rather grand voice. "Permit me to introduce you to 'The Spinsters Guild'."

· · ·

Thanks for reading this story! This is just the beginning of a fun journey with the four slightly imperfect ladies who are looking for husbands! Emily has to figure out how to help them and Lord Havisham is going to have to really work to help her!

My first series, The Duke's Daughters, is also about ladies looking for husbands! Those were the days! You can check it out here The Duke's Daughters

MY DEAR READER

Thank you for reading and supporting my books! I hope this story brought you some escape from the real world into the always captivating Regency world. A good story, especially one with a happy ending, just brightens your day and makes you feel good! If you enjoyed the book, would you leave a review on Amazon? Reviews are always appreciated.

Below is a complete list of all my books! Please check out my books on my Amazon Author page!

www.amazon.com/Rose-Pearson/e/B079CRBHDX

The Duke's Daughters Series
The Duke's Daughters: A Sweet Regency Romance
Boxset
A Rogue for a Lady
My Restless Earl
Rescued by an Earl
In the Arms of an Earl
The Reluctant Marquess (Prequel)

A Smithfield Market Regency Romance
The Smithfield Market Romances: A Sweet Regency
Romance Boxset
The Rogue's Flower
Saved by the Scoundrel
Mending the Duke
The Baron's Malady

The Returned Lords of Grosvenor Square
The Waiting Bride
The Long Return
The Duke's Saving Grace
A New Home for the Duke

Love and Christmas Wishes: Three Regency Romance
Novellas

Collection with other Regency Authors
Love at the Christmas Ball
Love, One Regency Spring

Please go to the next page for a preview of the first book
in The Duke's Daughters series, **A Rogue for a Lady**!

Happy Reading!

All my love,

Rose

A SNEAK PEEK OF A ROGUE FOR A LADY

PROLOGUE

"*A*re you quite ready?"

Amelia Seaworth, first daughter to the Duke of Westbrook, looked at herself in the mirror. She barely recognized her own reflection, taking in the beautiful dress she was wearing and the glow of happiness in her eyes.

"Yes," she murmured, rising to her feet. "Yes, I believe I am ready."

Harmonia, her youngest sister, smiled at her, tears sparkling in her eyes. "My dear Amelia," she whispered, blinking rapidly. "I do not think I have ever seen you look so beautiful."

Amelia smiled back and went to embrace her sister, holding her close for a very long time.

"I shall miss you," she said, hoarsely, as her emotions began to run wildly through her. "I do not know what I shall do without you, in fact."

Harmonia sniffed indelicately and pulled her lace handkerchief from her pocket as she stepped back, shaking her head a little. "Nonsense," she said, a wobbly smile on her face. "You will be so happy in your new home that I am quite sure you will not miss us in the least!"

"Well, mayhap I shall not miss Jacintha and Jessica *quite* so much," Amelia replied, a wry smile on her face as she thought of her two other sisters who were, at times, a little trying. "But you, my dear Harmonia, have been both a sister and a friend to me. There are times I can hardly believe we are so many years apart, for you have wisdom beyond your years. How I shall miss your company!" Tears threatened, even though Amelia practically burst with happiness and she was forced to pull out her own handkerchief and dab delicately at her eyes.

For a few minutes, the two sisters tried to get their emotions under control, laughing at one another's efforts to stop their tears, only for more to fall from their own eyes. Eventually, Amelia felt able to put her kerchief away and, glancing at herself in the mirror, saw that she looked quite well regardless of her tears.

"I am so happy for you," Harmonia said, as she delicately placed the veil over Amelia's head. "I know that he will make you very happy.

"Indeed he will," Amelia replied, a small smile on her face as she adjusted the veil. "A marriage with love can only be happy, I think."

Harmonia said nothing, glancing away from Amelia as she fiddled with the locket around her neck.

"You must promise me not to do anything foolish, Harmonia," Amelia said, firmly, grasping her sister's hand to get her full attention. "Swear it to me. I cannot leave you without knowing that you will, at least, come and speak to me before you do anything."

There was a long pause but, eventually, Harmonia nodded. Letting out a long breath of relief, Amelia smiled and patted her youngest sister's hand. "Good, I am glad. And it means you will have to come and visit me very often."

"As often as I can manage," Harmonia promised, as a rueful smile tugged at her lips. "After all, with you to be a married lady, the responsibility of finding a suitable husband now falls to me."

Amelia chuckled. "I do not think papa will rest easy until we are *all* wed."

Harmonia's smile faded. "Is he very sick, do you think?"

There was a short silence. "I do not know," Amelia admitted, quietly. "Papa can be tired and need to rest, but that does not mean he is ill. It simply means he is getting a little older, although that gout of his does flare up from time to time." Her heart wrenched as she thought of leaving her father's home, aware that she would not be able to care for him in the way she had been used to doing. "You must look out for him. Encourage him to rest whenever he is tired and make sure he eats well."

"Not too much brandy, then," Harmonia replied, the atmosphere lifting at once as she laughed.

"Yes, precisely," Amelia agreed, chuckling to herself as she recalled just how many arguments she had been forced to have with her father over his penchant for the best French brandy. "Although I am glad to know he is happy about my marriage. It would not have done to have him disappointed in my choice."

Harmonia smiled gently. "You need have no concern in that regard, Amelia. Our father is more than content. In fact, I believe seeing you in such a happy state has made him quite satisfied." She smiled at Amelia and lifted one eyebrow, her gaze running over Amelia's dress. "Well," she said, a little more briskly. "I think you look quite the picture of perfection, Amelia dear. We do not want to keep your husband to be waiting! Shall we go?"

Amelia turned to give herself one last look in the mirror, knowing that this would be the last time she would leave her bedchamber and leave her home. Her new bedchamber and new home would be with her husband, and life would be very different from what she had been used to.

"Yes, we should go," she said, softly, a smile spreading across her face as excitement began to run through her. "I can hardly wait to say 'I do'."

 *ix months earlier*

Lady Amelia Seaworth sighed happily to herself, settling into the window seat with her newest novel. Below her, the streets of London were busy with carriages, couples walking arm in arm and even a few street urchins, but Amelia did not give them much attention. She was far too eager to begin her new book.

However, Amelia was not about to have the peace she craved. No sooner had she opened the first page than the door to the library opened and her father, the Duke of Westbrook, came in.

"Amelia? Are you in here?"

Managing to abstain from rolling her eyes, Amelia let out a small sigh and came down from the window seat, leaving her book there. Hopefully, she would be able to return to it soon enough.

"Yes, papa?" she asked, smiling at her dear father. "Are you in search of me for some particular reason?"

Her father did not return her smile, making Amelia grow a little anxious.

"Indeed I am," he replied, gesturing to a seat by the fire. "Come now, sit with me. I have something I must discuss with you."

Goodness, this is serious indeed, Amelia thought to herself, her book now entirely forgotten. Hurrying to sit opposite her father, she settled her hands in her lap and looked at him in eager expectation.

"Amelia, I had the doctor visit me before we left for London," her father began, holding up a hand as Amelia began to exclaim at once. "It was nothing serious, I assure you. Just a little trouble with my gout."

"Oh," Amelia murmured, flopping back in her chair in relief. "Is that flaring up again? I had not known."

Her father grimaced, his gaze drifting away from Amelia and towards the fire. "I confess I have kept such trifles from both you and your sisters. You already have enough to do, stepping in where your mother ought to be, particularly with Harmonia. She was just a child when your dear mother passed." His gaze softened as he thought about his lost love, making Amelia's heart tear. Clearing his throat, he smiled and dashed a faint tear from his eye. "I know you are a strong woman and you do take very good care of me, Amelia, but there are some things that I need not concern you with."

"Regardless, I should know when you are feeling unwell, father," Amelia protested, gently. "You know how we all care deeply for you."

His expression softened. "Yes, I am well aware of that, Amelia. That is precisely what I wish to talk to you about."

A fluttering came into her stomach as her father's expression grew somewhat serious. His dark green eyes lost their humorous gleam as he ran one hand through his thinning grey hair.

"I have decided that you each need to find yourselves a husband."

Amelia blinked, staring at him. "Whatever do you mean?" she asked, a little breathlessly. "You have always left us to ourselves to make such a choice."

"And mayhap I was wrong in doing so," her father answered, gravely. "For who is going to care for you when I am gone?" Amelia opened her mouth to protest that her father would live to see a great many days yet, but he shook his head to silence her, clearly not finished speaking. Amelia was forced to lapse into silence, biting her tongue as best she could.

"Seeing the doctor today confirmed to me that I am not a particularly well man," he continued, heavily. "Besides, I am getting older." He gave her a half smile, his expression almost rueful. "I have tried to deny it for a great many years, but the march of time continues on. It is time you and your sisters married so that I can be sure you are all happy and settled before I pass on.

Amelia shook her head, refusing to accept what her father said. "No, papa, you are too harsh on yourself and much too melancholy."

"Within the year, Amelia," her father interrupted,

not listening to a single word of her protest. "You are all to be engaged or wed by this time next year."

Amelia was rendered speechless, almost unable to accept what had been said. By next year? The thought was preposterous!

"Did you really think we came to London simply for a holiday?" her father asked, softly. "It is the height of the Season, Amelia. You and your sisters are all out, therefore there is no reason you should not enjoy these few weeks, with the intention of securing a proposal."

"And I am to be first," Amelia spluttered, aware that, as the eldest sister, it fell to her to lead the way. She had been out for some years and, at the age of four and twenty, had thought she might spend the rest of her life as a spinster. After all, she was practically on the shelf but being the daughter of a Duke might give her a little more time to find a match. Not that she was particularly keen on the idea, however.

Her father shrugged as Amelia struggled to contain her shock. "I confess that I hate the thought of you all leaving my home and my company, but it is best this way. And yes, as you are the eldest, it falls to you first. You must lead by example, Amelia." Leaning a little closer to her, he searched her face. "I need to know that you will go into this with a willing spirit, Amelia."

Amelia wanted to rebel, to tell her father that she simply was not ready to find a husband, that she was quite content here, but the earnestness on his face prevented her from doing so. She could not deny him this, not when he was clearly worried for his daughters.

"If I must," she muttered, sitting back and pressing a

hand to her brow. "But it will be a man of my own choosing, father. I cannot be forced into matrimony."

The relief he felt was evident. "But of course," he replied at once, smiling at her gratefully. "Just to know that you are, at least, *looking* for the right gentleman takes a great deal of worry from my mind."

Amelia nodded absently, not quite sure how she was meant to find the right kind of gentleman when she had given very little thought to love and matrimony these last few years. In truth, she had spent most of those years caring for her father and ensuring that her sisters were not left to run wild. When their mother had died some years ago, it had fallen to Amelia to run the household and she had grown very content with her role in life. She had not considered her long-term future, even though she had always been aware that there was a little confusion and uncertainty over who the estate might fall to, once her father died. He had always seemed so robust and hearty, even with his occasional attacks of gout but it was clear to her now that he considered his life drawing near to a close – even though she did not agree with such a thought, of course.

"Now," her father continued, interrupting her fast flowing thoughts. "I have tickets secured for the four of you to Almacks for tomorrow night. Your cousin, Lord Luke Darnsley, will accompany you, given that my health requires me to be abed early these days."

"To Almacks?" Amelia repeated, surprised. "Goodness, father, you have been busy!"

He chuckled. "You are not the only one with a determined spirit, Amelia. Have you never thought where you got your determination from?"

Amelia could not help but smile. "I suppose you are right," she murmured, getting to her feet. "I had best inform my sisters."

Reaching for her hand, her father squeezed it gently. "You are very good to me, Amelia. You need not tell them of the urgency to wed if you do not wish to. Once you are married, the others will follow suit, I am quite sure."

Bending to press a kiss to her father's brow, Amelia pressed his hand gently before quitting the room, her heart heavy. Not that she would reveal such a thing to either her father or her sisters! Amelia was determined to put a brave face on things, even though the very thought of finding herself an eligible and worthy gentlemen filled her with anxiety.

"Ah, I am glad you are all still here," Amelia smiled, putting on a bright expression as she walked into the drawing room. Jessica was busy with her embroidery, Harmonia was reading quietly and Jacintha was writing something at the desk in the corner. They each looked up as Amelia entered, aware that she had only just taken her leave to read quietly in the library.

"Is something wrong?" Jacintha asked, putting down her quill. "You look strained."

"No, nothing is wrong," Amelia assured her, as cheerfully as she could. "The reason I have returned to you all is that father has just informed me that we are to attend Almacks tomorrow evening."

A stunned silence filled the room for a few seconds before each sister burst into questions, practically running towards Amelia who felt quite overwhelmed by it all. There were questions about dresses, what they would wear, who they would dance with, who would be attending, who was going with them, who would introduce them....the questions went on and on until Amelia, feeling quite weary, extricated herself from her sisters and went to sit down in one of the chairs. Of course, they followed, although it was Jacintha and Jessica who continued firing questions at her whilst Harmonia began to study her quietly.

"I do not have all the answers for you, I'm afraid," Amelia protested, holding up her hands to stem the flurry of questions. "I am only telling you what father told me."

"We are to find a beau, then?" Jacintha asked, hope flaring in her eyes. "I had thought father might have every intention of us enjoying a Season when he suggested a trip to London! After all, I am twenty and Jessica is two and twenty – it is high time we found ourselves husbands!"

Amelia thought quickly about how best to present what her father had said without informing her sisters about the urgency of her father's request for them to wed. "You are quite right, Jacintha. Father has decided that it would be best for us all, in time, to wed. And one cannot wed if one does not meet eligible gentlemen!"

"And where better than Almacks?" Jessica finished, giggling wildly. "Oh my! I must go this very moment to look through my new dresses. I am quite sure I will never find one to wear!"

"I will go with you!" Jacintha exclaimed and, much to Amelia's relief, they left the room together.

Harmonia let out a long breath, relaxing in her chair. "Goodness, Amelia! This has come as something of a surprise. Father has never been particularly keen on allowing us to mix with London society before."

Amelia nodded, her lips twisting a little in a rueful smile. "He thought to protect us, I think. After all, daughters of Dukes are particularly eligible, particularly with the inheritance we shall each receive. He did not want us to fall head over heels with rakes who have nothing but a shilling or two to rub together, even though they keep up every appearance of being just as wealthy as ever!"

Harmonia did not smile. "He intends for us each to wed, then," she said, thoughtfully, still studying Amelia. "That must be something of a trial to you. I know how settled you are."

"It came as a surprise, that is true," Amelia answered, slowly. "Yet I gave my assurance to papa that I would do as he asks. It is to bring him a little relief, I think, to know that we are all settled."

"But you must be the first," Harmonia commented, her sharp eyes piercing Amelia's calm demeanor. "After all, I am but nineteen so have some time before I must find a match – but I can tell that you are not as settled as you appear."

Amelia smiled sadly. "You have always been able to see what I really feel, Harmonia. Yes, I am not settled in the least. I would rather stay here with father, continuing in my role as it is. But, it seems, that is to be taken from me."

There was a short pause.

"But should you marry, you have the prospect of

having your own family and running your own house-hold," Harmonia pointed out. "It is not all bad, Amelia."

Amelia sighed heavily, knowing that her sister was right. "I shall try and make the best of it, I suppose. After all, what else can I do?"

"You can find a beautiful dress that sets off your eyes and makes you as lovely as can be," Harmonia declared, rising to her feet and catching Amelia's hand so as to pull her from her chair. "Come now, sister dear. Let us find you just the most perfect of dresses for Almacks tomorrow!"

CHAPTER TWO

"Come, come now! We must not be tardy!"

Amelia glanced up to see her cousin, Lord Luke Darnsley, enter the room in something of a flustered state. He was in his usual smart attire, his dark blonde hair neatly tied back at the base of his neck and his cravat absolutely impeccable. All in all, he looked quite dashing, were it not for the sharpness of his tongue and the way his eyes darted from place to place.

"We are quite ready," she said, in as pleasant a voice as she could manage. "May I thank you for accompanying us, Darnsley. We very much appreciate your kindness."

Luke did not reply, simply grunted and gestured towards the door of the drawing room. The sisters walked through one after the other, although Luke followed after Harmonia leaving Amelia to walk behind, alone.

The carriage ride was a quiet one, for no-one felt much inclination to speak in their cousin's presence. He was not an unkind man, but rather a man who had something of a sharp tongue and could often mock his cousins should they behave in a way he thought ridiculous. Even Jessica and Jacintha were silent, although Amelia knew they were both utterly thrilled to be attending Almacks. She also noticed that her cousin's eyes continually strayed towards Harmonia. Of course, second cousins married quite often, but Amelia did not think they made a particularly good match. Harmonia was kind and gentle, always aware of what was going on and making sure to aid where she could. After all, she had been the only sister who understood the difficulties Amelia faced in being the first one required to marry! Luke, on the other hand, appeared distant and aloof. No, they would not suit at all, even if her cousin could not take his eyes from her sister!

Once they had arrived at Almacks, Amelia stuck close to her sisters and cousin. After all, as much as none of them wished to dance with him, he was the only one who could introduce them to anyone else! As their chaperone, Luke held something of a large responsibility which Amelia was not quite sure he particularly wanted. Regardless, she stayed by him, nodding to first one gentleman and then another.

For the first hour, Amelia felt quite overwhelmed. There were so many new acquaintances to greet and, given the presence of four new young ladies to society, it seemed as though they were greatly in demand. Amelia's dance card was filled almost immediately, although each gentleman only signed his name to one dance, which was something of a relief. She saw that her sisters were much the same as she, relieved that she would not have to stand guard over them all evening. They were under Luke's chaperonage and, with their dance cards full, she did not think any of them could do anything untoward. Besides which, she had lectured Jacintha and Jessica on their expected behavior, threatening no more balls should they disappear, even for a moment, with an unknown gentleman. Her sisters had been quite put out that she thought so little of them and had told Amelia so, which, in all honesty, had come as something of a relief to Amelia. It told her that they would behave with all propriety and not lose their heads, as she had been worried they might do. However, as she watched them each take to the floor – with poor Harmonia coupled with cousin Luke, Amelia could not help but feel a twinge of anxiety. Her own partner, a Lord Dalrymple, was soon by her side and Amelia had no more time to be anxious, caught up in the dance.

"Amelia!"

Utterly exhausted from having danced four dances in a row, Amelia was delighted to see her longtime friend Miss Claudia Michaels, approaching her with a broad smile on her face. Claudia was a friend from home but had come to London for the season with her parents. Amelia had not even thought that she would come across her, particularly with the crush of people in the ballroom.

"Claudia," Amelia murmured, pressing her hands. "How good to see you."

"I must confess, I am a little surprised to see you here!" Claudia exclaimed, her eyes sparkling. "I did not think your father particularly cared for the Season."

Amelia gave her friend a wry smile. "Alas, it seems I

am to find myself a suitable husband – as are each of my sisters," she replied, heavily. "And where best but London town?"

Claudia chuckled. "Where else, indeed? Well, I can see that you have made something of an impression already, given the number of names on your dance card!"

"Indeed, although I am glad for a short respite," Amelia laughed, still feeling overly warm. "It is such a crush in here!"

"This is the way of things," Claudia replied, grimly. "How we are to find an amiable, respected gentleman amongst such as this, I am never quite sure."

"Is it truly terrible?" Amelia asked, knowing Claudia would be honest with her. "I do not find myself particularly inclined towards matrimony but it appears to be the deepest wish of my father's."

Claudia nodded, slowly, well aware that, with no sons to follow him, Amelia's father was left without any other option but to ensure his daughters married well. "I can understand that he would wish you all to be comfortable and without concern," she said, softly. "Yet, I will confess that it can be difficult to find just the right kind of gentleman. There are so many rakes and rogues amongst them all, although they hide themselves well." She shook her head, the light in her eyes dimming just a little. "I had a gentleman wish to court me and I did find him quite delightful, I must say. However, it has now become apparent that he is short on funds and only wishes to wed me in order to add to his own coffers."

Amelia grimaced. "That is just what I worry about. We each have a good inheritance."

"And you are the daughters of a duke," Claudia reminded her, lifting an eyebrow. "Be careful, my dear."

Amelia was about to promise that she would be more than careful when Jessica came hurrying towards them, all of a flurry.

"Amelia! Amelia – oh, good evening, Claudia."

Claudia chuckled. "Good evening, Jessica. Is something the matter?"

"Oh yes, something terrible has occurred!" Grasping her gown, she indicated a small tear at the bottom. "The gentleman I was dancing with trod on my gown! Can you believe it?"

Amelia eyed the rip in the gown, sighing inwardly. "Well, at least you know he is not a proficient dancer!"

"You must fix it!" Jessica exclaimed, sounding horrified that Amelia did not intend to do anything. "I cannot be seen with such a thing!"

Claudia put a calming hand on Jessica's arm. "Have no fear, there is a cloakroom present where maids are ready with a needle and thread." She laughed, indicating the way Jessica should go. "After all, yours is not the first torn gown!"

Jessica's relief was palpable and, grasping Amelia's arm, thanked Claudia before making her way in the direction she had indicated. Amelia, resigned to going to help her sister, thanked Claudia as she was dragged away.

"For heaven's sake, be careful!" she exclaimed, as Jessica hurried up the steps. "You need not drag me so!"

Reaching the top of the stairs, she wrenched her arm from Jessica's grip, only to lose her balance as Jessica continued to hurry away. Her foot wobbled at the top of the stairs and, for a horrifying moment, Amelia thought she might fall headlong down the staircase.

A strong hand grasped her arm, righting her quickly and pulling her away from the stairs. Amelia collapsed against a firm chest and strong pair of arms, only to blush deeply with embarrassment and step away.

"Are you quite all right?"

Glancing up at the man, Amelia felt her stomach swirl with a sudden awareness of just how handsome her savior was. "Yes, indeed," she mumbled, not quite sure where to look. "I am so terribly sorry for inconveniencing you."

The gentleman chuckled, his brown eyes warm and welcoming. "Not in the least. Any chance to be chivalrous, I say!"

Amelia could not help but laugh, the mortification she felt already beginning to ease. "In this case, you were very chivalrous, I'd say. I thank you." Looking up at him inquiringly, Amelia decided to be bold. "I'm afraid I do not know your name. Might I ask it, given that you are my savior?"

The gentleman grinned, his dark brown hair catching the candlelight as he bowed. Amelia saw flecks of gold and bronze and found, much to her surprise, that a flurry of butterflies appeared to have made their way into the pit of her stomach.

"Arthur Ridlington, Marquess of Northfell," he answered, in a deep, rich voice. "I am at your service, although I must beg to know your name also." He looked at her with a curiosity in his eyes, his gaze flickering from her eyes to her lips and Amelia curtsied at once, so that she might hide her flaming cheeks from his view.

"Lady Amelia Seaworth," she murmured, finally lifting her gaze back to his. "My father is the Duke of Westbrook."

Interest filtered into his expression. "I see. And is he here with you this evening?"

"No, unfortunately, he is not in the best of health at the moment. My cousin, Lord Darnsley, is here with us."

His smile broadened. "Us?"

"My three sisters and I," Amelia explained, growing more comfortable with his company with each passing moment. "I am the eldest of four." Glancing over his shoulder, Amelia gave a slight shrug. "I was being pulled along by my sister to fix a small tear in her dress when you caught me."

"Then I shall not keep you," he replied, stepping to one side. Amelia made to move past him, her heart beating a little more quickly as she passed, only for him to catch her arm.

"Forgive me," he murmured, his eyes burning into hers. "I know this is very untoward, and I am quite sure you are engaged for the rest of the evening, but I don't suppose you have a single dance remaining?"

A rush of heat crawled up Amelia's spine as she held up her dance card, finding it almost impossible to speak.

"One," she rasped, her skin prickling with awareness. "I have one left."

"Wonderful," he murmured, catching the card in his hand. "I would like to put my name down there, if I may?"

Mute, Amelia nodded, aware of just how close he stood to her. She could smell a wonderful mixture of pine and cinnamon, her senses swimming as he pressed her hand for a moment before stepping back.

"I very much look forward to our dance, and to know you better," Lord Northfell murmured, a light smile on his lips. "I shall see you again presently, Lady Amelia."

"Thank you, my lord," Amelia managed to say, finding that her legs struggled to move as she continued towards the cloakroom. Who would have thought that a single chance meeting would have sent her into such a tizzy! Lord Northfell was handsome, of course, and particularly attentive in asking her to dance with him, but she could not allow herself to be so caught up with him after only one meeting!

What is next for Amelia and Lord Northfell? Check out the rest of the story on the Kindle store. A Rogue for a Lady The Duke's Daughters Boxset is available with five full-length stories of Amelia and her sisters. Try it! The Duke Daughters

Made in the USA
Middletown, DE
16 February 2021